Fwishi'shi

by Kelci D Crawford

This project is partially funded by an Arts Commission Accelerator Grant made possible through support from the Ohio Arts Council, the National Endowment for the Arts, The Chapman Family and other generous supporters.

Fuloos Abieris lived alone in a home by the sea.

His home was not like the homes of the other people further inland. His home had been carved out of a cave on the side of the cliff, carved by his great-grandfather, and passed down from father to son until, finally, Fuloos inherited it.

He missed his mother and father every day. But his home had history. He didn't want to leave it behind. It had so many stories within its rocky, dusty walls. Some stories he knew, because he lived them. Others he knew because his father and grandfather told him.

Fuloos loved stories. So much so that he began to tell them.

Unlike the other writers who lived in the town close by, he did not write fantasy or science fiction, romance or suspense. He did not write mysteries, either, unless the stories he wrote had them. He wrote the stories of other people - biographies. Nothing fascinated him more than hearing or reading the stories of other people. Real people. People who lived in flesh and blood and led brave or quiet or outrageous lives.

Thankfully, people noticed how good he was at writing them. So people bought his books. And then people asked him to talk to real people. So he did. And people listened to him talk to real people.

Seabank, as a little town of fewer than 500 people, had settled near the cliff by the sea. And if you asked anyone in Seabank who the most famous person in town would be, they would say, "Fuloos Abieris, no doubt." The radio show he hosted had him talking to strangers so listeners could hear their stories straight from the source. And people listened. Not just in the town of Seabank - people as far as 500 miles away could tune in, on radio or podcast. Fuloos Abieris had listeners from as far as Inlai, on the other side of the Blue Mountains.

He did not host his show in his ancestral home - it didn't even have electricity. Everything in his home had to be lit with either log fires, candles, or storm lamps. He had been incredibly lucky that his father had the foresight to install running water when Fuloos had been a young, downy boy.

No. To do his radio show, he would hike his way to the top of the cliff thanks to Oloos pass - named after his great-grandfather - and then ride his bicycle into town, to the WB49 radio station.

Today, on his way to the station, he noticed something peculiar. Odd, even.

He stopped his bike at the intersection of Main Street and Igvo Way, feeling the wind dance through the vanes of his crest feathers. And he saw the townsfolk gathering on the sidewalks, staring at the same thing he was seeing.

There, in front of the café, sat a limousine.

Now, he and the residents had been used to tourists. Tourists were the driving force of Seabank, keeping their small town alive and the shops running. But Fuloos had not seen a limousine in person since his college days so many years ago.

He wondered aloud, "Why is this here?"

Standing next to him was Avery Makekis, a Capuchin man standing a bold four and a half feet tall, his tail curling around his ankles. He brushed a speck of sand off his tacky blue shirt, patterned all over with palm trees and beach balls. "Some fancy folks came in," Avery said. "Mayor's talking to them right now in Perly's - " Perly's was the cafe the limousine parked in front of. "I think it's some kind of magazine feature?"

Next to Fuloos and Avery, a gray cat woman approached. She wore glasses at the end of her nose, which only made her wide green eyes look even wider. This was Misses Breanne Ridgeway, the oldest woman in town. "I heard from my friend Jeanie who works in the Mayor's office that some magazine out of Inlai wants to feature our town in their local vacation spots or something like that."

Fuloos nodded, though this confused him further. People came to Seabank to do articles on this town all the time. Mostly to focus on the history of the place, or the Indigenous people still residing there, or chasing the stories about the sea nymph who lived off the coast. None of the people before had come in a limousine.

Avery asked, "Do you know why the special treatment, ma'am?"

"No clue," Misses Breanne admitted. "Jeanie only told me what she knew."

Fuloos checked his watch. Though he had red and red-orange feathers of various lengths on his body, the feathers on his wrists and forearms were the color of burning logs - dark brown, nearly black. So his watch stood out on his feathers. He had an hour and a half before his show began. His original plan had been to go into the café and write a few more pages for his next biography project. But the limousine and the unusual mystery derailed his intentions.

He pedaled up to the bike racks in front of the café, Perly's, and locked his bicycle into a free space. Then he went inside. To his surprise, no security tried to turn him away.

He did, however, see the Mayor sitting with a small crowd on the far right side of Perly's. The party had pulled two tables, each originally intended for four people, and pushed them together to seat the seven people present. The Mayor, a human with dark brown skin and thick fingers and a bald head, spoke at length with a Peregrin man, a red hawk man (Fuloos' feathers bristled at the presence of both of them), two Dalmatian men, and two other humans. One had brown skin, like wet rock on the beach, and the other...

The other human had their back to him, so all he could see was their long, dark red hair. He could see their hair extend down to the middle of their back, loose and straight, draped over the back of a lilac purple dress.

He turned away, lest anyone think he had been staring. He passed by the scattered tables and chairs, only one or two others of which were occupied with dining customers. He came to the counter, not sitting on one of the barstools yet.

Holly, the hen woman who waitressed at Perly's, approached him. Today her golden comb, long and extending to her chest, had been pulled back by a red ribbon. The red matched the red on the walls. At least, the red walls that were visible under the multitude of framed pictures.

"What'll ya need, hun?" Holly asked.

Fuloos replied, "The usual, please. And anything you've heard about…" He blocked away from the new arrivals so he could point to them without being seen by them.

Holly clucked and turned around. "Not much I can tell from that, I'm afraid," she said. She popped the strainer off the espresso machine and poured the beans for Fuloos' usual order - a mocha with cookie shavings and cream. Fuloos had a sweet tooth - or, a sweet beak - and was not ashamed to admit it.

As Holly made the drink, she said, "I can tell ya' now, they're talking about a feature. But our town is a little backdrop for what they're plannin'."

That raised the feathers on his crest with intrigue. He sat up straighter. "'Backdrop'? Is this a movie?"

"Nah, nothin' that big," she said. She popped the filter back in, set a mug down under it, pressed a button, and let it roar to life. Holly and Fuloos waited for the machine to finish in an effort to not shout over it. The machine was old. Any sense of subtlety the espresso machine was capable of died the same day it lost its first fuse.

After a while, the machine ceased its grind. Holly resumed while making the final touches for the order. "It's not a movie. It's some kind of fashion shoot for a new label out of Inlai. Something to do with Wings of Peace, I think."

He knew of Wings of Peace. One of his biography subjects, Hawley Blue-Feather, founded the organization with Orpex the Bald. The goal of Wings of Peace was to establish peaceful unity between the Feathered peoples of Veri Peninsula. They emerged after the Gold

Talons - a pro-hawk hate group - started becoming more vocal and more visible in major cities. It did not surprise him, then, that Wings of Peace would be interested in Seabank. Besides its charming sea-side cliff scenery and walkable town (and Fuloos himself), the town's biggest claim to fame was its founding - as a refuge for Little Feather people and other minorities that people like the Gold Talons and their predecessors, the Uberfalkes, would persecute. Yes, a handful of Hawk people lived in Seabank, but they were White Owls and Rabbithops, ethnicities who were considered "not hawk enough" by whatever standards the extremists set.

Holly passed Fuloos' order to him and said, "Don't be surprised if they wanna' talk to you, hun."

He said, "Thanks, Holly," settled onto a barstool, and got to writing.

*

Roisin sat, utterly bored, at the table with the Mayor and the Wings of Peace committee.

She had been brought there to speak as the model the committee chose for their project - Wings of Peace released a new line of fashion as part of their Caw Back campaign, and they needed a model. Of course, she volunteered - how could she not? Wings of Peace had a very important mission that resonated with her and her boyfriend, Blue, a Peregrin man. (Admittedly, it surprised her that the committee accepted her - a human - as a model for this project. But the committee's argument had been that "humans are the neutral party, so having a neutral party model our new line will help us reach our audience and turn neutral people into supporters.")

Except here, now that the business had been largely handled, the topics of conversation moved to other things, such as streaming shows she didn't watch or movies she had not seen. So she let her eyes wander around the cafe.

It had its charm. Red walls covered in framed photographs taken over the decades - many photos were black and white, and some betrayed the first era of color photos with their pale pastel hues and fuzzy edges. Any space on the wall not covered in photos opened into a window, letting in bright sunshine.

Roisin noticed the bird man at the counter, sitting on a barstool. He was, at first glance, a Little Red Feather, but even though he sat, she could tell he stood taller than other Red Feathers she met. He wore a dark blue vest over a light brown, long-sleeve shirt. The sleeves had been rolled up to his elbows, showing off short red feathers on his forearm that led down to dark-brown, nearly black wrists, hands, and fingers. His slacks, though tan, had trace elements of sand along the bottom cuffs. She watched him adjust the round glasses that rested at the top of his beak, and he continued scribbling into his notebook, unaware of being watched.

Something about him made her think she had seen this bird man before...

"Roisin," Blue said next to her.

"Hm?" She turned back to him. "Sorry. Thought I recognized somebody."

Blue, her Peregrin man boyfriend, raised a brow ridge. "I thought you said you've never been to Seabank."

"I haven't. Which is why I'm puzzled."

Blue glanced over to the Red Feather at the counter, then he turned to the Major. "Who is that? Do you know them?" he asked.

The Mayor said, "What?" Looked, and said, "Oh!" He said to Blue and Roisin, "That's Fuloos Abieris. He's one of our local celebrities. Writes marvelous books."

Something clicked in Roisin's memory. "Didn't he write the biography of Hawley Blue-Feather?"

"I wouldn't be surprised if he did. You should ask him yourself - he loves to talk to people."

Blue remarked, "I'm sure he does."

Roisin shoved an elbow into his arm. "Not all Little Feathers are the same," she said.

"I didn't say anything!" Blue said, hands up.

"Well I'm going to ask him," Roisin said, and she got out of her seat and left the party. The conversations resumed as she did.

*

Partway into his writing, Fuloos heard a young woman clear her throat next to him. He set his pen down and turned in his seat.

It was the human from the large group from Inlai. She had skin the same shade as the pale sand, eyes the vivid blue of the sea. Across her nose, freckles dotted. And not knowing what to do with her hands, she pulled them behind her back. "Excuse me for interrupting," she said to him. "But I just noticed you and thought I recognized you. Did you write 'Dancing on Feathers of Joy: the Hawley Blue-Feather Story'?"

Ah. A fan. It had been a while since he bumped into one casually. He smiled and said, "I did. I take it that you read it?"

She smiled so brightly at him. "In one day! I hadn't read a book like that in years!"

"What did you like most?" he asked. He could feel his interviewer tendencies begin to come up - turning the conversation to the person talking with him, so he spoke about himself as little as possible.

This young woman either did not notice or did not say anything about it. "How can I narrow it down? If I had to pick just one thing, it's how you show Hawley empathizing with people who are so extremely hard to empathize with. It's one thing to tell the reader; it's another to show that empathy in action, you know?"

That answer warmed him up better than the coffee ever could. He nodded, and said, "I'm glad that resonated with you. So you know about her mission with Wings of Peace?"

She nodded, enthusiastic to speak with him now. "I'm actually here with Wings of Peace. We wanted to come here for a photo shoot for a new project!"

"Oh?"

So he listened as she spoke about Wings of Peace and their Caw Back initiative, and the release of new apparel that promoted speaking out against hate and promoting messages of peace.

She stopped at one point and said, "I'm so sorry, I'm just babbling and you're trying to do your thing."

Fuloos said, "You don't have to apologize."

His watch beeped. When he looked at its face, it betrayed that he had thirty minutes before his radio show began.

"Oh," he said, and turned the alarm off. "I'm so sorry, but I need to get to the studio."

"Studio? Oh! Right, you host a radio show." And then the young woman said, "Could I - we, maybe - join you to listen in?"

He had opened his saddle bag and tucked his notebook and pen inside, but paused before he could slide off his seat. He said, "Uh-hm...you mean listening in, in person? At the studio?"

The young woman's eyes fell to the floor and her shoulders tensed up closer to her ears. "Actually, forget it. It's an impulsive ask - "

"Well, I don't want to keep you from your company, either," he said to her, flicking his beak towards the party she had been sitting with.

The young woman took one glance at her group, waved, and turned back to him. "Actually, that gives me an idea...if you're willing to hear it, of course!"

*

So that's how Blue Pernico sat next to his girlfriend, Roisin, watching a radio show through a pane of glass.

He never actually saw how radio shows got produced. So it fascinated him to see what happened on the other side of the glass. He watched Fuloos take a seat at a desk with a multi-jointed microphone hooked into the wall. The red bird man picked up a pair of headphones and put them on over his ears. Another person - a producer, presumably - sat at another desk across from him, with headphones of her own, operating a three-screened computer. The woman, a human with black hair and pale-white skin in eyeglasses as big as coffee cups, gave Fuloos the thumbs-up.

Fuloos returned the gesture. Then the woman raised five fingers and counted down.

Roisin sat next to Blue, enraptured at the process unfolding before them.

He smiled a little. In truth, things between Roisin and Blue had been difficult. Mostly because work would call for him and force him to leave for long stretches of time. He would try to make it up to Roisin with gifts - flowers, fruit, candy, or letters - but it didn't make Roisin less sad. He would come home after those absences to a Roisin who mourned and wouldn't leave the bed until he climbed in next to her.

Here he was, though, sitting with her as the radio show began. She even held his hand and listened to the interview. Blue had been told that this host, Fuloos, would conduct new interviews every other week and speak with prominent people. Today's guest was an Elephantine author present during the Pocolico Factory Riots seventy years ago. The guest had to be called in over the wireless, of course, as the guest in question resided in Yaloy - which sat even further away from Seabank than Inlai.

As Blue listened to the interview, something struck him about it.

Back at the cafe, he had teased about Little Feathers only because of his own parents - two Little Feathers, Blue Jays, who adopted him as a downy boy. His parents, and the other Little Feathers he grew up listening to, were always talking. Mostly about other people, but always chattering, whistling, singing, and harping. He didn't know a moment's quiet until he started his internship at Usbad magazine a few years ago and got his own apartment.

The thing that struck him here, however, was Fuloos himself.

"...That's odd," he mused to himself.

Roisin heard his muttering. "Hm?" She turned to face him.

"...He's not talking a lot, is he?"

"Who?"

"Fuloos."

Roisin patted his thigh. "Well, he IS interviewing Pat'Ba'an - " the guest author, "so Fuloos is listening."

Blue said nothing. It just surprised him that a Red Feather would listen more than talk. That was all.

He didn't say anything more about it, though. He wanted Roisin to enjoy the experience.

*

Fuloos did not see Roisin or her boyfriend, Blue, again until five months later.

During that time, their campaign with Wings of Peace had been a success. Fuloos continued his work. The season slowly transitioned from spring to the heat of summer. And then the steady crispness of fall came on the wind.

Fuloos still lived in that ancestral home built into the cliff. In fact, he had to begin stockpiling wood and lamp oil for the winter. No trees grew on the cliff or on the beach, however. So he had to go into town and trade for it with Magukin McGuiness, one of the Beaver people who managed the forests southeast of town.

Of all the things he had to trade for wood, the beavers loved seashells. That, and clams. Thankfully, Fuloos' grandfather showed him how to harvest clams and fish from the sea, so he had plenty of both and the means to acquire more for trade.

He had just returned from a trip to town. Avery the Capuchin lent his pickup truck and his hands to help Fuloos bring firewood back home. So the two packed up the pickup's bed with wood and Fuloos' bike and drove back to the top of the cliff. Once there, Fuloos parked his bike in the three-sided shelter, and the two began to unload.

This entailed Fuloos descending the Oloos pass to the bottom of the cliff. As he went, Avery would load a platform at the top of the cliff. And then, thanks to a pulley system Fuloos' father had installed years ago, Avery would lower the platform down to Fuloos. Then the birdman would unload the logs and stack them neatly in a recess by the entrance of his home, send the platform back up, and the process would begin again.

As the two brought the pulley system up and down to move the day's winnings...well, that's when Fuloos saw her.

At the beach at the bottom of the cliff, she stood with her back to the men. Fuloos could recognize the narrow shoulders and the way the dress held her frame as the wind blew. Her hair had changed from the last time he saw her - where once it had been long, brown, and straight, it was currently bright red and cropped shorter, going only down just past her shoulders, and it curled like the sea's waves.

While he stood at the base of the cliff, he did not notice the pulley system's platform lowering until it hit the top of his head.

"Sorry!" Avery shouted from the top of the cliff.

Fuloos rubbed his noggin and unloaded the platform. As soon as the platform returned to the top, however, he turned around and approached the young woman roughly forty feet away from the cliff.

The waters of the sea lapped at her feet and ankles. She stared out over the water and did not notice Fuloos right away. The scene reminded him of *her*, someone he hadn't thought of in a long time...

"...Excuse me," he said to the human woman before him.

She pulled her gaze away, and for a moment her sea-blue eyes kept him there. "...Mister Abieris?" she asked him.

"Just Fuloos," he said. "Are you...Roisin?"

"...I'm surprised you remember me."

"Well, you do look a little different from last I saw you."

"Wha - oh." One of her fingers curled around a lock of her hair. "Yeah. I decided to stop straightening and dyeing my hair. The chemicals just kept damaging it."

"Hm." He had been wearing a light jacket that day, and here he could see Roisin hugging her arms over her chest. So he took his jacket off and draped it over her shoulders.

The gesture startled her out of her daze. She hooked her fingers into the fronts and said, "...Thank you."

He nodded. "I have to help Avery get the rest of the firewood down. But when we're done, I'll come back to you to check on you again." With that, he returned to the task at hand at the base of the cliff.

He did not know this, but Roisin watched him until he and Avery finished their work.

*

Avery waved goodbye from the top of the cliff. Fuloos waved back. And then Avery turned around and got into his pickup truck.

As the engine roared and drove away, Fuloos returned to Roisin's side on the beach. He asked her, "What brings you back to Seabank?"

Roisin's eyes, which had been watching him approach, darted to the side at the question. She tucked a lock of hair behind one ear and said, "...I...needed some time to myself."

"Oh. Well if you need me to - "

"No! Not like - that's not what I - " Flustered, she sighed and buried her face in her hands. Through her fingers, she said, "...I'm thinking of breaking up with Blue."

Not knowing what else to say, Fuloos held her shoulder. "...Why don't we go inside and have some tea? You need something warm...besides my coat."

*

Roisin had never been inside a cave home, so she didn't know what to expect.

She didn't expect the walls to be painted. Instead of the red rocks of the cliff, the back wall of the kitchen and dining room had been painted a bright sea green. Recesses had been carved into the wall to house plates, pots, tea kettles, jars of herbs and spices, baskets - she even spotted a couple of cookbooks next to the fireplace. The fireplace had wire shelves installed in it to hold pans and pots as the flames rolled.

Fuloos pulled a dark blue kettle from a recessed shelf, filled it with water from a nearby pot, then set the kettle on the lowest wire shelf over the fire. Roisin watched him go about his work.

"...Do you have a refrigerator?" she asked him.

Fuloos turned to face her. "There's no running electricity here. But there's a cellar in the very back of the house that stays cold all year."

Roisin stared. "...Did you say 'no electricity'?"

"Indeed. And don't drink any water from the faucet. Something got into the well. I asked Avery and Tookis - " Avery's brother - "to fix it tomorrow."

As Fuloos walked back to the table and took his seat near Roisin, she said to him, "But you're - I'm sorry, but you're a famous author. You have a radio show! Why live like this? You must have the means to get a house in town."

The smile he gave her betrayed his sympathy. "It's not a question of means. It's a matter of heritage. I inherited this house after my father passed and left it to me. Just like his father left it to him, and my father's father before him. This house has been part of our family since my great-grandfather, Oloos, carved this place."

Roisin went quiet. Her eyes drifted around the room, and Fuloos' eyes moved with hers. He indicated trinkets and treasures scattered throughout. There, on the top shelf across from them, sat the plates his grandmother commissioned from an artist friend. Next to those, a mug his grandfather had made for his wife. Next to the stove, his own mother's cookbook, complete with coffee stains, earmarks, and scribbles in the margins for substitutions and corrections. Finally, her eyes, and his, landed on the tea kettle in the fireplace, a gift Fuloos had gotten from his coworker at the radio station, Ursula.

The tea kettle did not whistle yet.

Fuloos held one cheek in rest and leaned an elbow on the table - the table his great-grandfather had built out of driftwood and wood palettes, with parts replaced over the years as it aged.

Roisin leaned forward in her seat. "Can you tell me more?" she asked him.

"Hm?"

"About this house. About your great-grandfather. Why here? Why a cliff house?" The light in her eyes flashed with curiosity. She gasped. "Are there *mermaids* here?"

He chuckled. "If there are, I have never seen any. They must be very good at hiding. Or not attracted to birds."

This made her giggle - a sound he never heard before from her. "Well, that's too bad for them."

He could feel the feathers on his cheeks and neck rise a little. The tea kettle whistled quietly, the roiling boil just beginning. "Let me get that," he said in a hurry, and he rose from his seat to fetch the water.

Once he had the tea situated, he passed a red mug to Roisin. He held his own sea green mug and sat down across from her. "So how long will you be in town?" he asked.

Roisin held the mug tenderly. The steam rose in place. "...Just a few days. Maybe a week...I don't know yet."

"Why the hesitation?"

She sighed through her nose. "I don't know. I came here to clear my head. Think about what to do. Blue is..."

Fuloos recalled Blue, Roisin's Peregrin boyfriend. "If you don't mind, I want to ask about his limp. Has it gotten any better?"

Roisin blinked. "...He's always had that."

"Oh. I'm sorry."

She waved a hand. "You didn't know. It's not the leg that's bothering him. It's his being gone so much that bothers ME."

"He's always gone?"

She nodded. She recounted to him the times before the two met Fuloos - how Blue would promise to be at a party or a date, but bow out at the last minute because of work. How Blue would try to send flowers or other gifts as an apology. And how these absences and presents became more frequent after the two had met Fuloos.

The disappearances became so frequent that Blue didn't even appear when Roisin needed him most - after the death of her grandmother. And what happened after Roisin called him out on it?

Blue had sent a flower arrangement for the funeral. He himself had not been present.

Recounting this, Roisin's eyes stung and watered. She took in a sharp inhale and held a hand over her mouth to hide.

At this, Fuloos got out of his seat, knelt beside her, and held her against him. As if like a tidal wave, Roisin sobbed into his shoulder, holding him tight so the sorrow would not wash her away.

"I'm sorry," Fuloos cooed to her. "I'm sorry you had to go through that." He thought of his own grandmother's passing, and how his family and family friends had been there for him. To not have someone you love present for something like that...that was something he would not wish on anyone.

It took a long time for Roisin to take deep breaths and settle. When she did, Fuloos pulled a handkerchief from his pocket and gave it to her. He wiped a stray tear from her cheek while gazing into those ocean blue eyes of hers, overflowing with grief and relief.

Roisin hiccupped. "I'm sorry," she said. "I didn't mean to just dump that on you like that - "

"Never apologize for your feelings," Fuloos told her. "But my grandmother's spirit won't forgive you if you don't have a sip of that tea before it gets cold."

That gave her the chuckle she needed to break the spell of sadness. "...Thank you," she said.

"Of course."

*

Blue panicked as soon as he saw the note on the kitchen counter.

He knew that things had gotten worse between him and Roisin, no matter what he tried. But then he saw the letter she wrote to him. A letter stating that she would be gone - she didn't know how long - to clear her head and reconsider "some things."

His gut told him that one of those "things" was their relationship.

It sucked because he wanted her to be happy! And there would be times that she was. But those times did not last very long - in fact, they ended as soon as he had to leave to do his work. Being a photographer meant having to take a gig while the getting was good - too long of a wait, and the gig would pass to someone else.

And he needed those gigs! He needed the work to get paid, to get bills and student loans paid, to get the things that would make him and Roisin happy. And he had a lot of catching up to do - three years of internships made him rack up a lot of debt that set him back on his timeline.

Finding consistent work or a full-time, long-term job was impossible to snag in his industry. He had to keep hustling. But it felt like no matter how hard he worked or how many gigs he booked or how much he got paid for those gigs - it felt like other people still had the leg up over him.

Not just literally, because of the stupid limp he had since birth. It just...hurt him to see his coworkers and friends have things he still couldn't have because he couldn't afford them. The nice apartment in a not-shady part of town, lunch dates, Friday night bar hops - he wanted these things for him and Roisin, but he could not provide them. The gigs just couldn't pay for them. Sometimes the gigs even got in the way!

More than anything, he hoped Roisin would be patient. Just a little while longer and then they could do those things guilt-free.

But then he saw the letter. He was taking too long - again.

He had to DO something.

He picked up his cell phone and called Stacey - a mutual human friend of theirs. As soon as he heard Stacey pick up, he babbled, "Stacey! Roisin's gone and I don't know where she is! Did she tell you anything?!"

"Wait, what? She's gone?" Stacey finally caught up.

"Yes!"

"Oh shit! She told me she had been thinking about taking a vacation, but I didn't think it was THIS soon."

"A vacation?" Did Roisin lie to their friend?

"She had some unused vacation days. She was talking about using them to go back to Seabank."

"...Seabank?" Why there? He tried to think of what could possibly have been in that village that would get Roisin to pack up and disappear for who knows how long.

"I know, right?" Stacey said on the other line, breaking his chain of thought. "I thought it was weird to go to the middle of nowhere. But I guess she didn't want anybody calling her or texting her. Remember how Nathan and I had a bitch of a time trying to reach you out there? We had to resort to freaking email. Nobody uses that anymore."

Blue let her babble for a second as he pondered the implications. Roisin left for a place to deliberately separate herself from her friends. From HIM.

He cut into her talking and asked, "Can you tell me where she's staying there?"

"I have no idea. You'd have to ask Joel - " another mutual friend, someone Roisin knew since before he started dating her. "I'm pretty sure that if she had train ticket info, she would pass it along to them."

It took a few minutes to get off the phone with Stacey. Once she got talking, it was hard to get her to stop. But after he (blissfully) ended the call with her, he dialed Joel.

Joel answered the phone with a chipper, "What's up, my good bitch?"

Blue told him of the situation. "Did Roisin share anything with you about where she was staying? Or anything else?"

Joel gasped on the other line. "Oooooh, honey, are you gonna' sweep her off her feet on the beach all like 'it's been you all along' and shit?"

"YES." If that's what it took to save their relationship, that's what he would do.

And so, Joel said, "Ok. Give me just a sec to pull up the itinerary she texted me..."

*

Fuloos glanced out the rectangular window. "Oh! It's getting late. Are you staying in town?"

Roisin nodded. "Mmhmm. At the Cuddly Nook."

Oh good. That was the bed and breakfast Misses Ridgeway operated. "Here, let me walk with you back to town."

"Walk?" Roisin glanced out the window and saw the sky's deeper shade of blue. "But if we do that, it'll be dark by the time we get there!" She frowned. "If we do that, would you have somewhere to go? I would hate to see you go back home alone at night."

This was quite a pickle. He didn't expect Roisin to stay so long here. But then again, they had lost track of time while talking and enjoying tea (and each other's company).

Then a thought occurred to him. "Let me call Avery. He can give you a ride home."

"'Call'? I thought you said there was no electricity."

"No need for it," Fuloos told her. He stood up from his seat and said, "Follow me if you would like to see a Seabank secret."

*

So Fuloos stepped out of the cave house, out to the middle of the sandy beach. He instructed Roisin to stay by the entrance of the rock house, though she didn't know why. She also didn't know why he had nothing in his hands. She did, however, watch him roll up his sleeves.

It startled her to see such defined forearms on a birdman like Fuloos. He raised his red arms, cupped his dark brown hands by his face, and let loose a high-pitched whistle she could hear even from fifty feet away.

He must have been so loud that the whole town of Seabank could hear him, even a mile away!

*

Fuloos called out in the whistling language a message that translated to, "Calling on Avery!"

He waited a moment. Then - in a way that startled Roisin as she watched from the entrance of his home - the two of them could hear a whistling call back.

The message translated to, "Avery's busy! It's Patan!" Patan was Avery's roommate.

"Patan!" Fuloos replied in the whistles. He asked, in this language, if she could drive to the cliff to give someone a ride back into town.

He heard a reply back. The message translated to, "They're at your house?"

"Yes," he replied via whistling. "She needs a ride to Misses Ridgeway's. Can you do that please?"

The waves rolled softly onto the sands. The high tide encroached on Fuloos' feet and swept around his bare ankles. Then the reply came in the wind. A high series of whistles translated to, "I'll be there in ten minutes."

He whistled a series of notes that meant a sincere form of thanks. And he returned to Roisin.

Roisin stared at him in wonder. "What was that?"

Fuloos smiled, the crest feathers on the top of his head rising a little. He clicked his beak and said, "Faiji - it's a whistling language used since my great-grandfather's time."

"Oh wow." Roisin didn't even notice the wind brushing past her face until a curling lock of hair fell onto her cheek. She brushed it back behind her ear and asked, "Does everyone in town use it?"

"Just about. But a lot of the children don't speak it. Most don't want to learn it."

"What? Why?"

He shrugged. "Why whistle when you could call or text? I suppose that's their reasoning."

"But that's so neat!" She gasped. "Wait, what did you say exactly?"

"Just that you needed someone to drive you back to Misses Ridgeway's. The driver said she would be here in a few minutes." He held an open hand to her. "Would you like me to walk you up to the top?"

*

Blue waited at the train station. He wanted one of the cushioned seats that ran in a long oval shape in the waiting area. Those things looked long enough to lounge or sleep on. But other people had that idea first.

The only train he could find to take him to Treeta - a stop closest to Seabank - ran at midnight.

He had never been on a train before. But Seabank had no airport, and Blue didn't own a car. He only knew one person with a car - Steven - and he was out of town that weekend to Juli for a show with his band.

So, the midnight train it had to be.

The announcement came on the overhead, loud and full of feedback and grain. "Attention passengers of Train 46 - " that was his train, "your trip will arrive shortly on the platform. Please make your way to Platform 2 and wait for the conductor's signal. Please allow passengers arriving to disembark first."

Blue let the other instructions roll on the overhead as he picked up his duffel bag and made his way - slowly, thanks to his limp - to Platform 2.

His leg hurt him immensely since his panic that afternoon. So he had to resort to his cane. He also had to resort to using some of his emergency funds to pay for this trip. He hated having to do that, but this was an emergency for him.

It took another twenty minutes for the passengers to line up by the train, for the previous riders to disembark, and for him and his fellow riders to get on.

Once the train got rolling, he couldn't sleep right away. The panic came to him again.

Would Roisin even want to see him when he arrived? But then, why wouldn't she? Wouldn't she have been happy to see him? Knowing that he had to buy a ticket to get to her - to book a room somewhere? To stop everything to see her again?

Eventually, the rocking of the train took over his senses. His eyelids weighed heavily, and after the panic at last turned to exhaustion, he succumbed to sleep.

*

Patan, a tuxedo-patterned cat-person, pulled her four-door car up to the side of Misses Ridgeway's bed and breakfast. The bed and breakfast was Misses Ridgeway's first house her husband built, and she did her best to take good care of the place, even after his passing. Of course, she ran the two-story house with some assistance. Patan herself would assist, often by driving Misses Ridgeway's guests, usually to the train station. (The station had a connection to Treeta to the northeast, and Treeta served as the main nexus for transit in the peninsula.)

This time, Patan drove this guest, a model by the name of Roisin, to Misses Ridgeway's bed and breakfast and home-away-from-home.

Roisin opened the back door of the car, as she had been sitting in the rear. She asked the tuxedo cat woman, "Do I owe you anything?"

"Nah," Patan said, looking in the rear-view mirror to look at her. "You're good to go. Tell Misses Ridgeway I'll be back tomorrow to pick up Mister Hort in the morning. That'll be payment enough."

"Thanks," Roisin smiled at her, closed the door, and made her way inside.

Misses Ridgeway sat in the living room parlor, knitting something large and pink. Her large, bespectacled eyes spotted Roisin. "Oh! Good. I heard Fuloos asking Miss Patan to give you a ride. I'm glad you made it back safe and sound."

Roisin gawked. "You could hear that?"

"Of course! Faiji isn't exactly subtle, dearie. If you want to keep something private, keep it to a whisper, not a whistle."

Roisin had to remember that. "Oh! Before I forget, Patan wanted me to tell you that she will be stopping by tomorrow morning to pick up someone."

"Oh good! I'm glad Mr. Hort has a ride to the train station." As Misses Ridgeway spoke, she did not stop knitting the whole time.

Roisin took a step closer and asked, "Would you like me to get anything for you?"

"Oh no, no, you're perfectly alright," Misses Ridgeway said. She took a second to brush her plentiful whiskers. "Help yourself to tea and cookies, if you like. I baked these fresh before dinner."

Roisin sat on a plush chair beside Misses Ridgeway. The chair, like the other chairs, had a white and red floral pattern that, by some miracle, did not clash with the floral wallpaper in the living space. Anything that had not been covered with fabric or handmade tablecloths had been made of dark wood. Or, in the case of the tea tray on the coffee table - a light wood.

Despite herself, Roisin poured a cup of tea, even though she had some already at Fuloos' home. She asked aloud, "Misses Ridgeway, how well do you know Fuloos?"

"Fuloos Abieris, you mean?" When Roisin nodded, Misses Ridgeway gave it some thought. "Well...I knew his grandfather. I only met his great-grandfather once or twice. Mister Oloos liked his privacy. Obviously, or else he wouldn't have carved a house into that cliff." She chuckled to herself, then flipped her work around to continue knitting.

Roisin picked up her teacup and a gingersnap cookie. "But Fuloos himself?"

"Mmmmm," Misses Ridgeway purred. She closed her large eyes thoughtfully. "...I suppose I've known him the longest of anyone in town. Outside of Avery or Ursula."

Roisin didn't know how to gracefully bring this question forward, so she just asked directly. "Was Fuloos ever married?"

Misses Ridgeway's knitting stalled. Her purring slowed until it ceased. "...He nearly married once."

The teacup nearly fell from Roisin's hand. "...How long ago was this?"

"Hmm..." Misses Ridgeway's triangular ears pulled back. "I'm not sure I should be the one to talk to you about this, dear."

"Was it bad?"

"Bad how?"

"Like, was the other person...not good?"

Misses Ridgeway huffed. "Well, I don't know if I can fairly judge that. I CAN tell you that the two of them had very different ideas of what raising a family would look like. But that's all I can tell you. You would have to ask him." Her knitting sped back up.

Roisin sat back in her chair to ponder this. "...Is it because he still lives in that house?"

"That his great-grandfather had built? Possibly. I know most modern women don't like how rustic it is. That reminds me - did Fuloos get someone to check on his well?"

"He mentioned something about somebody taking a look at it tomorrow."

"Oh good. I should send that young man some cookies anyway."

"You should!" Roisin said, smiling as she took a bite from one of the cookies on the tray. "These are delicious!"

Misses Ridgeway slowly blinked and then chuckled.

*

By the time Blue arrived, the clock struck 5 am. But that was his first stop. It would be another hour from the Treeta connection to Seabank itself.

He didn't know if he could get more sleep during the connecting ride. As soon as he got on the Treeta train to Seabank, he glanced out the window to catch the view.

It amazed him that he had gone from the flatness of his home city to the base of a large mountain range. He could see the trees changing colors as he and the train sped past. The sky, cut off in places by the mountain peaks, held no clouds, so the bright morning sun came down on everything outside of his window.

He was the only person in his car on the train. Despite the clacking of the wheels and the occasional train horn blaring into the wind, he felt alone in a way unfamiliar to himself. Not even his thoughts came to keep him company in the seats nearby. And he didn't know what to make of this sensation.

So he kept his eyes on the view outside the window, and tried not to let the feeling sit in his chest. He was unable to sleep for the rest of the ride.

When he arrived, he felt sluggish and tired in a way he had never felt before. It was even worse than his college days when he pulled all-nighters. He wondered how this was possible when he actually managed to get some sleep on the first leg of the trip. Was it the emotional exhaustion and not the physical?

Well, he made it to the Seabank train station in one piece - physically, anyway. His mind felt unfocused, but he had to shake the feeling away. The first thing he needed to do was find the bed and breakfast Roisin was staying at.

Once he stepped away from the platform, he exited the building and saw a mint green, four-door sedan parked by the steps. An aging golden cockatiel person stepped out from the back of the car. A tuxedo-patterned cat person came out of the driver's seat, opened the trunk, and pulled out a carry-on suitcase covered in stickers and scuff marks. She passed this bag to the older birdman and said, "Have a safe trip, Mr. Hort!"

The birdman thanked her and slowly ascended the steps, pulling the bag behind him as it clacked on each step.

The tuxedo cat girl spotted Blue and said, "Hey, mister! Need a ride?"

"That depends," he said. "Do you know where the Cuddly Nook is?"

"Sure do! Just came from there. Hop on in. Let me get your bags."

The cat person - Patan, he learned - drove him to a cozy, two-story house with bright and colorful violets and daisies and daffodils by the front porch. Someone sat on the front porch, an older Basset hound man with his pants pulled high on his waist and a pipe in hand. He raised the pipe at the car as it pulled up to the house.

Patan helped Blue out of the car and up the steps. She wished him a great day, and then drove away.

So he walked into the bed and breakfast. The first thing he saw was a staircase that led upstairs, and a desk to the left of it. At this desk, an older, gray-furred cat woman with large glasses had been busy tidying up keys and note papers. As soon as she spotted Blue, she said, "Good morning, young man! How can I help you?"

"Yes, do you have a spare room I can stay in please?"

"I sure do, but it's not quite ready yet. I still need to change the sheets and make it nice for you. If you're willing to wait about ten, fifteen minutes, there's breakfast ready in the kitchen. Help yourself while I get everything situated."

He thanked her and did just that. He didn't realize how hungry he was until she said something. So he moved to the right, passing through a very bright and rosy living space, to the back of the house, where the kitchen had no door to close it off from the rest of the house. He passed through the entryway and saw the bagels, the toaster, the stacks of pancakes, the coffee pot, the bananas and other fruit, and knew immediately what he needed in his system right that second.

*

Roisin rose that morning with an odd sense of relief - something she hadn't felt in a long time. It must have been her time with Fuloos. She never realized how much she needed that valve of grief to be opened and released. And yet, thinking about the previous day's events, she felt so calm and secure with the older birdman.

She meditated on this while brushing her teeth and getting dressed for the day. She hadn't packed much for the trip - she tried to keep everything in one suitcase - but she kept one of her favorite dresses with her: a blue, calf-length sundress with clouds patterned all over. She slipped it on, brushed her hair, and went downstairs for breakfast.

However, she only made it halfway down the stairs. She turned her head to look into the living room and saw...

Blue.

He had his back to her, but she knew that figure and that cane anywhere. Wait, he was walking with a cane? Did his leg get worse? Why was he here with a plate full of blueberries and a cream cheese bagel? She didn't tell him where she was going! She didn't tell anyone but Joel -

Did Joel talk?

Blue scanned the room for a chair. Likely he was looking for one with an ottoman so he could raise his aching leg.

She turned back around to head up the stairs, until she heard from the living room, "Roisin?"

Blue had spotted her.

The two locked eyes for a moment. Blue had this expression in his eyes like relief, his crest feathers rising a little at the sight of her.

Her panic kicked in. And she bolted out the front door.

She could hear something in the living room falling and Blue calling out for her. She tried to ignore it and ran down the porch steps, down the sidewalk and turning a sharp right down an alleyway. She just kept running until -

She had looked over her shoulder to make sure she hadn't been followed, but ran into someone. The two collided, but the other had not been knocked over. The person she hit held her shoulder.

"Roisin!"

She gasped when she saw it was Fuloos who held her shoulder. He saw the expression on her face and how short of breath she was and he said, "What happened? What's wrong?"

Then she realized what she did. She had just seen her boyfriend - someone who had to get a ticket to get here, to SEE her - and she just ran out on him.

Roisin felt her eyes sting. "Fuloos, I'm such an idiot."

Utterly confused, Fuloos pulled Roisin in for a hug. Without thinking, she pulled her arms tight around him. "Deep breaths," he cooed. "Deep breaths. You're ok."

She tried to inhale slowly but it just came in sharp in her mouth, like a knife. "Blue is here."

She didn't see his face but could hear the confusion in his tone. "Your boyfriend?"

Despite herself, she nodded and rested her chin on his shoulder. "I don't know how, but he found out where I was staying. I didn't tell him anything, I don't know how he found out."

Fuloos let go of the hug and stepped back to look her in the face. "...You didn't tell him you were coming here?"

She shook her head. Realizing how foolish that sounded, her eyes welled up with tears.

"...Did you tell *anybody*?" he asked.

"Just my best friend Joel. But why would they tell Blue?"

She expected Fuloos to ask why she didn't tell Blue anything. That even though she was considering breaking her relationship with him, that she should have told him where she was going. It's what good girlfriends would have done -

But he didn't do that. He let one hand trace down her arm until his hand held hers, and he said, "Why don't we find a quiet little booth at Perly's? Then you can tell me everything."

*

Blue had dropped his plate without thinking and rushed to the door. But by the time he even got to the porch, Roisin was gone.

"Roisin!" he shouted for her. But he heard no reply.

The Basset hound man on the porch spoke up. "Ah, young love," he said. He tapped the ashes out of his pipe. "Not that it's any of my business."

Blue said nothing. He just turned back around to get back in the living room parlor and clean up the mess he made.

Why did Roisin run from him? He knew the note she left for him, he knew the implication that she wanted space away from the city - and by extension, from him. But to run away at the first sight of him? What did he do wrong?

He picked up his fallen food and set it on an end table. Then he made his way to the kitchen to get napkins and pick up some of the cream cheese stains off the rug.

The gray old cat stepped out of the kitchen and said, "Now what bit that little girl in the butt so hard she had to run like that?"

He choked back a chuckle - he certainly didn't expect THAT out of the older cat woman. "I don't know," he said. "I thought she would have been happy to see me."

"Oh! You know her?"

"...I thought I did."

*

Fuloos and Roisin sat at a booth in the back corner of Perly's. The booth seats had tall backs to them, and the side window only looked out on an alleyway covered in vines with white flowers, which covered a faded mural. So in short, there was no risk of someone spotting them, outside of Holly.

Holly took their breakfast orders and scuttled back to the kitchen. She clucked at Gallus, the rooster man who worked in the back. This, of course, set off a series of clucks and bakaws that only other chicken folk would understand. Fuloos only caught a handful of words, and only because he had come to Perly's so many times.

Roisin listened to the back and forth and asked so only Fuloos could hear, "...Can the chef speak Common?"

Fuloos shrugged. "I've never heard him use it."

"How do you work with people and not speak Common?"

"Common is a difficult language for the Gal folk to practice, so don't judge them too much."

"I - " realizing the tone of the conversation, Roisin shook her head. "I'm sorry. I didn't mean to sound rude."

Something seemed to glint in Fuloos' eye. He touched his fingers lightly on the rim of his coffee mug, and he asked Roisin, "So now that Blue is here without you knowing about it until now...what's next?"

Roisin stared at a spot of condensation on the table. "I don't even know. I didn't want him here at all. I wanted to be free of everything in Inlai so I wouldn't have to think about that life. I wanted space away to actually BE with my thoughts."

Fuloos' crest feathers raised up a little at a connection he made mentally. "Did you leave a note for him?"

Roisin nodded. She hid her face in her hands, propping her elbows up on the table, and huffed a defeated sigh through her mouth. "Lot of good THAT seemed to do."

"Do you remember what the note said exactly?"

Roisin said, "That I was going away for a few days and didn't know when I would be back. But I didn't want any phone calls, texts, or emails because I would be out of signal. I didn't want to see anybody I knew on this trip."

Fuloos leaned forward in his seat. "Roisin - forgive me for being forward here - but if you made it clear that you didn't want to see anyone...and Blue followed you, anyway?"

"THAT." Roisin let go of her face but did not lift her head, yet the slump in her shoulders turned to rigidity. "Oh my god. Now that you're saying that OUT LOUD..." She lifted her gaze to Fuloos.

Fuloos did not want to assume anything, though. "Does he ignore your boundaries often?"

Roisin snorted and leaned back in her chair. "You have to be around to break boundaries. I hardly ever see him. Except when he wants to be seen, apparently."

"Hmm..." Fuloos tapped his fingers on the rim of his mug, then looped his grip around the handle, lifted the mug, and took a sip. He said nothing right away.

Roisin scoffed. "During the whole relationship, I just wanted him with me more, and he was hardly ever there. But now that I don't want to see him, suddenly he wants to be with me? What is UP with that?"

Fuloos lowered his drink. "...Do you want to see him again?"

Roisin opened her mouth to say one thing, but it caught in her throat. Her jaw snapped shut and she huffed through her nose. She sank back into her booth seat. She folded her arms across her chest. "...I was hoping I wouldn't see him until I got back to Inlai."

"And when would that be?"

"Three days from now. But I can cancel the ticket 24 hours in advance if I want to stay longer. I wanted to keep my options open."

Fuloos gave a slight tilt of the head and blinked. "That's...I've not heard of anybody who would vacation here for longer than a weekend. Most people miss...well, let's just say Seabank is too rustic for some folks' tastes."

"But that's why I wanted to come back," Roisin said. She sat up straighter and uncrossed her arms. "I was here months ago and really liked not having constant notifications going off on my phone, or constant text chains or anything like that. I liked how people know people here - like, you know them by name and what they do and everything! Inlai is too big and too noisy for that. Everybody in Inlai is doing their own thing, and I wanted to get away from that."

"...Do you think Blue is going to bring that, now that he's here?"

Roisin looked away. A curling lock of hair fell over her eyes, which she brushed away and tucked behind her ear. "I don't think he could literally bring that kind of vibe. He knows as well as I do that there's no signal out here for our phones."

Fuloos did not want to ask this, but felt it necessary to do it. He leaned forward and extended a hand towards her. "...Do you think he plans on hurting you?"

Roisin gasped. "What? No! And even if he wanted to, he doesn't have the strength to do it, poor bean." Her eyes fell on her glass of water, which she had not touched. "When I left him, he was leaning really heavily on his cane. He must have been in pain since he got off the train..." She covered her mouth with one hand.

Right at that time, Holly came by and dropped off their plates - bacon, sausage links, and pancakes for Roisin, and a bagel and lochs for Fuloos. "Just holler if you need anything else," Holly said, and then walked back to the coffee pot when she saw that Fuloos needed a refill.

As soon as Holly left, Roisin asked Fuloos, "...Am I an idiot?"

Fuloos shook his head, even while spooning the lochs onto half of his sliced bagel. "Have you been honest with Blue up to this point?"

"I've always been honest with him."

"But you ran out the door as soon as you saw him. Is there something you don't want to tell him?"

"I mean..." she picked up her fork. "Is there a graceful way to say to someone, 'Hey, I'm thinking of breaking up with you because you're never around'?"

"How come you haven't said that to him?"

Roisin had slipped her fork into the pancake stack, then lifted the butter knife to slice a wedge. But at Fuloos' question, she paused mid-stroke. Then she lowered her arms and stared at Fuloos. "...How do you know the right questions to ask?"

Fuloos smiled at her with a twinkle in his eye. "Answer my question and I might tell you."

She huffed through her nose. As she resumed cutting the pancakes, she said, "...I'm worried about what he might say."

This, to him, seemed like a fair concern. "Have you fought before?" he asked her.

Roisin had to chew on her food for a moment while thinking about the answer. Eventually, as Fuloos ate his bagel, Roisin said, "...We've never really fought. We'd...disagree. Like, where do we wanna put the coffee maker in the kitchen sort of stuff. But that was all teasing and poking fun. We never..." she huffed and set down her silverware. "We never argued."

As she sipped her coffee, Fuloos set down his bagel and swallowed. "Have you ever wanted to argue?"

"Who WANTS to argue?" she asked in retort. She sipped her coffee.

"The answer might surprise you," Fuloos said. He thought about some noteworthy characters he had interviewed previously for his radio show. It had never been the lawyers or professional fighters who wanted to argue, oh no. The argumentative ones had always been other authors whose interests had been in the status quo and maintaining it for their own gains. Fuloos only ever ended one interview prematurely, and it was a combative twenty-something young man who wrote a book saying that Wings of Peace were extremists pushing anti-hawk agendas. Fuloos ran out of patience and ended the call in the middle of one of the author's rants. The rest of the program had been dedicated to the art of debate and how to engage meaningfully with others. It had been one of the few times Ursula got roped in to speak on air.

But Fuloos found it noteworthy that Roisin would ask this question. The question of "Who wants to argue?" It told him something of where she placed meaning in a relationship.

Roisin, for her part, ate her pancakes and sausage links in thoughtful silence. She looked ready to say something else, but something loud rang out in the kitchen. The sound was followed up by ruffled bakaws and clucks coming from Gallus the chef.

The noise made Roisin's brows scrunch up. "...Is everything ok?"

Fuloos stood a little from his seat to get a better look into the kitchen through the server window. He saw Gallus grab a bucket and rag and bend down out of sight. "Oh, he's fine," Fuloos said as he sat back down. "He made a mess, but he's fine."

Roisin relaxed back into her seat. She continued her breakfast. "So," she said. "...did you have plans for the rest of today?"

Fuloos had taken a bite of his lochs and bagel, so he had to finish that first. Then he said, "Just a visit to Jenny's to pick up some new books. For research."

Roisin leaned forward. "Research?"

Holly stopped by the table and refilled their coffee mugs. Both of them gave her a quick thank-you.

"I'm starting a new project," Fuloos admitted. "I just need to know who it should be about."

"Can I come with you?" She asked him.

Fuloos raised a brow. "...Do you want to talk to Blue first?"

Roisin shrank back in her seat. "...I'm not ready to yet."

Fuloos sipped his coffee but said nothing yet. On the one hand, he wanted to respect her wishes. Especially since she had been distressed so badly earlier. On the other hand, he knew things would only get worse if she dodged the issue. And he had a hunch...

He set his mug of coffee down. "... Jenny's isn't that far from here. We'll go after breakfast."

*

Jenny's Bookstore sat in the middle of Igvo Way, the same stretch where Perly's did its business. Jenny's Bookstore was not, however, run by a Jenny, but by an Ingrid Uveles, a human woman with thick, round glasses and curling brown hair always tied back into the bushiest tail.

No one in town ever recalled seeing her hair done any other way. She knit her own cardigans in bright, thick yarns and could answer any and all questions about books and their authors. In short, she was the perfect woman to run a bookshop in a small town with independent authors.

Fuloos and Roisin walked in, a small bell chiming at their entrance.

Ingrid lifted her head from her knitting, saw them both, and set her project away. "Morning!" she said cheerfully. "Who's this you brought with you today, Fuloos?"

Fuloos smiled. "Ingrid, this is Roisin. Roisin, this is Ingrid, the best bookseller I've ever met."

"Flattery will not get you a discount," Ingrid said with a knowing grin.

"It never does," Fuloos admitted. But he knew what did.

Roisin said, "Thank you. I've never actually been here before. Is this all new or used?"

"Yes," Ingrid said proudly. "We carry all of it. New, used, rare, indie, out-of-print. We manage to fit all of that in here."

"Really?" Roisin looked around. The space was, of course, packed with books, but it looked no bigger than a one-bedroom apartment back in Inlai. A ramp ran at a gentle incline from the store's entrance into the first row of bookcases, and signs hanging from the ceiling declared what sections were dedicated to certain topics. Offhand, Roisin could see signs for Stationery, Classics, and New Literature.

Ingrid grinned. "It only looks small because you're in the first house."

That got Roisin's attention. "...I'm sorry, 'First house'?"

"Yup! This store is built out of three houses all joined together. We're on the first floor of the first house. There's still two other floors up top. And each room in this store is dedicated to different genres."

Roisin's eyes lit up. "So...you have a room for Biographies?"

"Yup!"

"And an art room?"

"Yup! The art room has a closet full of puzzles, too, if you're into that."

"How do I get to the biographies room?"

Ingrid reached around a display on the front desk and pulled a map from a brochure display. "Here," she said. "Take this map. It has the whole layout of the store."

Roisin approached and accepted the map, staring in awe at the variety of rooms available. "There's a room just for local authors?" She gasped.

"Yup. You'll even find some of Mr. Abieris' books in there, too."

Fuloos quipped for Roisin, "Flattery will not get you a discount."

Ingrid chuckled. Roisin touched Fuloos on the shoulder, smiling, and said, "I'll be in the local author's room if you need me." And then she promptly dashed up the ramp and disappeared through a door on the right, her curly hair and bright dress bouncing as she did.

Ingrid watched her leave before turning to Fuloos. "She's not a new local, is she?"

He shook his head. "Just visiting on vacation. Said she needed a break from Inlai."

"Everybody needs a break from Inlai," Ingrid quipped. "That place has too much going on if you ask me. So how'd you meet her? Is she a fan of yours?"

"You could say that."

Ingrid raised a brow, but did not press further. "So," she said instead. "What brings you in?"

"Looking for some new material for research," he said. "I'm hoping to find some inspiration for my next biography while I'm here today."

"Have you ever considered doing one on a White Feather?"

Fuloos leaned on the counter. "Is there someone that comes to mind?"

"Maybe Chief Olohoolu?" Ingrid said. "I've only ever seen one portrait of the dude, and some hearsay from the White Feathers who come here once a month."

"That's...not much to go on."

"But challenge accepted, am I right?" Ingrid smirked.

Fuloos's eyes turned sharp and he grinned. "Color me curious, for certain. Now where did you see a portrait of this Chief?"

"In the 2816 copy of Tazzen's Gallery, volume 2. We have volumes 1 through 6 in the Art room if you wanted to start there. We also have a copy of White Feather Folktales in the History room. It has one or two stories about Chief Olohoolu and his daughters."

"Your taste and knowledge, as always, is impeccable."

Ingrid beamed with pride. "I know," she said. And as she bent back down to get her knitting, Fuloos took a copy of the map and set off for the History room.

*

The bell above the bookstore entrance rang as Blue stepped through.

Ingrid raised her gaze and set her knitting aside. "Hello!" she said, "What can I help you find today?"

Blue had been gawking at the overly crammed bookshelves before he noticed Ingrid talking to him. His falcon vision honed in on her and he said, "Actually, I'm looking for a person, but she's pretty likely to be here."

"Who ya looking for?"

"A young human woman. About yay tall," he gestured one hand about a head shorter than his own 6 and a half foot stature, "with curly red hair in a blue dress."

Before he could say a name, a look of recognition came to Ingrid. "Oh yeah! Her name was uh..." she snapped her fingers. "Roe-sheen, am I right?"

"Roisin, yes. So she was in here?"

A third voice came in. "Who's asking about Roisin?"

Rounding the corner came Fuloos with a stack of five books. One was as thick as a dictionary but the rest had less than 200 pages each.

Fuloos saw the young hawk man and said, "Ah! You're Blue, am I right?"

Blue's face lit up. "Hey, I remember you! You're that author she likes. Uh...Mister Abeer?"

"Abieris," Fuloos corrected gently. He set his book stack on the counter in front of Ingrid.

"Abieris, sorry. I only met you that one time."

Fuloos waved it off. "Quite alright," he said. He then turned to Ingrid, "I managed to find some books mentioned in the bibliographies of those initial books you mentioned."

"Well!" Ingrid said, "I'm glad I happened to have them!"

"'Happened to'? I'd think with how well they were placed that you got these specifically for me."

Ingrid gave a conspiratorial smirk to Blue. "This bird thinks he can tweet sweet nothings to me to try and get a discount."

Blue gave a polite chuckle. But Fuloos winked at her and said, "Oh, I know what will do the trick. Hold on to these for me, I'll be right back." He turned and left out the front door, the bell jingling as he did.

Ingrid turned to Blue and said, "So last I saw Roisin, she was headed towards uh...I think Biographies? Or the Art room, if you wanted to find her."

Blue had been watching Fuloos leave, but he turned to Ingrid. "At this point, I'm too curious. I wanna see what he's gonna do."

"Fair enough. This place is a maze, too." She leaned forward and took a map from the brochure display. She passed this map to Blue, who took it as she said, "This'll tell ya where everything is in this store."

He stared at it. "You need a map for a bookstore?"

"We're three houses all smashed together, so yes, you need a map."

He let out an impressed whistle. "Are there benches or chairs along the way? Cuz uh..." He tapped his cane twice on the floor.

Ingrid leaned over the desk and saw. "Oh! One sec, I have a collapsible stool I can get ya." She hopped off her swivel seat and ventured to a corner by the end of her checkout counter. She bent down and started digging through some things that made metallic or thumping noises as she moved.

The front door chime rang again. Fuloos had returned, carrying a tote bag full of something bulky but light. Blue took a peek inside and saw large skeins of bright, chunky yarn filling the tote bag to the top.

Ingrid stood back up straight and said, "Here we are!" She stepped around from behind the counter, revealing that under her cardigan and patchwork skirt, she had one metal leg. Her feet wore leather moccasins. In one hand she held something folded up into a bright green, two-foot square. She looked ready to say something to Blue until she spotted the tote bag in Fuloos's hand.

She squealed in delight. "Are those the new colors from Sheena's?!"

Fuloos nodded with a smile. "All alpaca wool, as well. She mentioned you had been eyeing these for some time."

Ingrid passed the contraption to Blue saying, "Take it take it take it." Her eyes stayed glued on the tote bag.

Blue set the map on the counter and took the contraption. As soon as he did, Ingrid's hands snatched the tote bag right up and she peered inside.

"I need that tote bag back, though," Fuloos said with patience.

Ingrid raised her gaze. "Like, right now?"

"Well how else can I carry out my books?"

"Right right, ok ok, one sec." She took the tote and ventured back behind the counter. "Is the receipt in the bag?"

"Yes," said Fuloos.

"Glorious." With that, Ingrid disappeared below the counter, making noise as she moved things around.

While she did, Blue turned to Fuloos. "So," he said. "Did you see Roisin in the store?"

"The craft store or here?"

"Here in the bookshop."

"Yes. She and I came in at the same time. She might still be in Biographies. That's where I saw her last."

Ingrid stood back up, receipt in hand. She began tapping keys on the register screen.

Blue asked Fuloos, "Did she seem...worried at all?"

Fuloos took one look at the young falcon man and saw the wrinkles under his eyes and the slump in his shoulders. And Fuloos said, "She's been worried since yesterday."

This made Blue's pupils dilate slightly, his crest feathers peeking up. "Since yesterday?"

Ingrid cut into their conversation. "Fuloos, ya need anything else?"

Fuloos looked at her and said, "Not today, thank you."

"That comes to $15.05 then."

Blue shook his head, his crest and cheek feathers fluffing up a little. "$15.05 for that stack?"

"It was quite a discount," said Ingrid. "But don't get too many ideas. Not everybody knows about it."

Fuloos pulled his wallet from his back pocket and dealt out a $20 bill. When Ingrid took it, he said to Blue, "Roisin has had a lot on her mind lately. I'm of the opinion that she needs to speak to you sooner rather than later."

The register rang as the change drawer slid open.

Blue leaned towards Fuloos, the grip on his cane tightening a little. "Is she..." he paused. "...Did she say anything about me?"

Ingrid gave Fuloos his change. As he tucked it into his wallet, he said, "She's done nothing but talk about you this morning."

"What did she say?"

As Fuloos tucked his wallet back into his pocket, he looked at Blue and his own crest feathers raised slightly. "...You two really need to speak to each other."

Blue raised the contraption in one hand and his cane in the other. "...Can ya please walk me to her? I can't hold a map."

Ingrid said to Fuloos, "I'll hold on to these for ya," and she pulled the stack of books aside and set them on a shelf behind her.

"Thank you."

"But if you get any more books," she said, "your discount won't apply."

*

Fuloos led Blue - slowly - round one corner and up a set of narrow steps. On the right-hand side sat a recessed bookshelf in the wall with a sign declaring "Camping and Hiking."

Blue tapped a knuckle to the sign. "It's like they put that there on purpose."

That made Fuloos chuckle.

Once they topped the stairs, they turned right and proceeded down a hallway. They passed one room on the left marked "Politics." They also passed a somewhat smaller room on the right marked "Sexuality."

At the end of the hallway, they saw a room on the left marked "Art." The room on the right had been marked "Biographies."

During their trek, they saw a handful of other customers browsing the shelves or sitting on the floor, reading books. Some were human, some were cat people or other Little Feather folk. But none were Roisin.

But then the two men turned to face the Biographies room.

Standing at the window, Roisin used the natural light pouring in from the street to read the beginning part of a book. Neither bird man could catch the title of her volume, but they saw how engrossed she was in the book itself.

Fuloos gestured for Blue to take a step in.

Blue recalled Roisin's reaction that morning to seeing him. So he whispered to Fuloos, "...Can you stay here for a second?"

Fuloos nodded.

With that, Blue cleared his throat and took a shaky step into the room. "...Hey."

Roisin lifted her gaze - she had been so absorbed she didn't hear anything from either man until Blue spoke to her directly. She spotted Blue first, and he could see Roisin freeze in place. She turned towards the entrance to the room and saw Fuloos watching them both.

Fuloos leaned one shoulder against the open door frame. He took off his glasses and wiped the dust from them with the bottom of his shirt. Fuloos was not a big man, but he had broad shoulders. And the house was small enough that Fuloos could fill the door frame.

So Roisin could not leave, unless she decided to open the window and leap out of the second floor. She closed her book quietly and cleared her throat. "...Morning, Blue."

Blue unfolded the contraption in his hand, which became a two and a half foot square box. He leaned and sat down on it, wincing a little as he did. Then he propped his cane up on the side and leaned forward slightly in his seat. "Sure would be nice if this place had an elevator," he quipped.

Fuloos smiled a little but said nothing. He knew the houses that made this shop were old.

Roisin lowered her eyes from Blue. "...I'm sorry I ran away," she said, her voice hushed. It came out nearly a whisper.

Blue had to ask, "Why did you run?"

"I..." Roisin looked fully away and out the window. The sun hit her hair just right so that her locks shone like afternoon rays. "I didn't think I would see you here."

"So you ran out the door?" Blue asked.

Fuloos stopped leaning on the door frame and took soft, slow steps down the hall. He lingered in the hallway between the Politics and Sexuality rooms, keeping an ear out but giving the couple their space.

"I'm sorry," Roisin said. "I panicked."

"You saw me and you panicked?"

Roisin started and stopped words coming from her mouth until she huffed and hid her face in her hands.

Blue leaned forward, even more concerned than before. "Roisin, what's really going on?"

A ginger cat woman stepped out of the Politics room with two books. She took a step towards the Biographies room but Fuloos stopped her and shook his head. His eyes darted towards the room in such a way that suggested, "Look but don't get too close."

When Roisin blurted out, "I don't think this is working anymore," the ginger cat woman made a face that said, "Ah." She gestured a 'thank you' sign to Fuloos, who nodded back to her, and she turned around and went downstairs.

"W-what?"

Fuloos wanted to step away so he wouldn't hear the conversation, but he also didn't trust Roisin to turn and run out the door right away. So he stood and listened.

Roisin sighed. "You're always gone when I need you, but the minute I need to step away, suddenly you want to be near me."

"You left with no warning! You didn't tell me where you were going or how long you would be gone. I was worried!"

"YOU were worried? You're gone all the time!"

"That's for work - that's different!"

"It's ALWAYS work!" Roisin's voice was rising. "It's ALWAYS rushing to catch the next big gig. What about us?"

"Why do you think I'm working so hard?" Blue's voice also rose. "I work hard to support us. To support you - to get you things that make you happy."

"I don't want 'things,' Blue! I - I want you to be around more. I'm so tired of waiting for you to come back home. I'm so tired of being left alone."

*

Roisin and Blue stared at each other for a long time in silence, broken only by the sounds of other customers in other rooms stepping on the old, wooden floor boards. After a while, Roisin broke eye contact to stare out the window, to focus on something else besides the growing lump in her throat. She pressed her fist to her mouth. Her other arm hugged around her chest.

For his part, Blue didn't know what to say right away. He hadn't expected Roisin's reaction, and he certainly didn't expect her to say she felt lonely. He felt his grip on his cane loosen as he lowered his feathered head.

"...I'm sorry," he said. "I never...I never wanted you to feel that way."

Roisin's eyes fell to the window seat, a faded, thin cushion on a wooden box, holding the book she had been flipping through. She stared, feeling the pull to get away. But her feet stayed anchored in place, her heart like lead.

Blue slowly got to his feet, using his cane to give him leverage. He took tired steps towards her, stopping to reach out to her to hold her arm. "But I'm here now," he said. "Both of us are here. We can use this like a vacation for the two of us. We can spend some time together here for a few days."

Roisin shook her head. She didn't make eye contact with him. "I hate this," she said quietly.

Blue let go of her arm. "...Hate what?"

"THIS," she said. "What you're doing right now. Because you'll only be around until the trip is over and then you'll be gone again."

"Roisin," he said, "I can't just quit my job - "

"I'm not asking you to quit your job, Blue!"

"Well what ARE you asking?"

"Were you even - " Roisin caught herself. She didn't want to yell, but everything in her wanted to. She turned and rushed out the door.

"Roisin!"

Roisin kept walking. Fuloos saw the look in her eyes and knew better than to stop her. He let her pass him to run down the stairs.

Blue stayed by the window. Even if he had the capacity to run at full speed, he was too confused and stunned to do so. He leaned one way as if to start going after her, and yet he stayed anchored by the window seat. He let his eyes drift to the book on the cushion. He picked it up and glared at it.

After a moment of silence, Fuloos stepped up to the entry into the Biographies room and watched Blue glaring at the book in his hands. "...What's that?" Fuloos asked him.

"...Roisin was reading this when we came in," Blue said. Holding onto it, he turned to leave.

"What are you - "

"I'm going to get this for her," said Blue, walking towards the door.

Fuloos did not move. "...Do you think that's what Roisin wants right now?"

Blue stopped.

The two men stood in silence as the words sank in. Blue's gaze drifted back down to the book in his hand. After a moment of contemplation, Blue turned in his spot and tossed the book back to the window seat. It plopped in place, closed, as if untouched.

The falcon man sighed deeply.

Fuloos stepped up to him and patted his shoulder. "...Why don't we get some coffee?"

Blue's eyes softened a bit, his crest feathers lowering. He relented with a tired nod of the head.

"Good," Fuloos gave him a pat and turned towards the door. "My treat."

"Oh, you don't have to do that - "

"I don't imagine the last-minute ticket to get here was cheap," Fuloos said as he paused in the doorway. "...It's fine. My treat."

*

The pair walked (slowly) up the slope of Igvo Way and turned right on Regis Lane to get to the Coffee Haus.

The Coffee Haus was a new addition to Seabank, being less than a year old as an establishment. So the white walls still needed art, planters, or more to make it truly cozy. In the meantime, the owner - a Pincher dog man named Burt Barkis - treated what few decorations available like minimalist installations on the walls. Floating shelves housed one or two props on each, and the light bulbs hanging from long ceiling cords had no adornments.

What saved this Coffee Haus were two things: the aroma of roasted coffee beans that permeated the air as soon as one opened the door, and Burt himself. Burt knew his coffee drinks. Even if someone from out of town requested a drink commonly seen at a chain store in a city like Inlai, Burt knew how to brew it. He also knew how to pick his people to help him behind the counter. He knew he was good at making coffee and very little else. Burt was a good, kind man. But he wasn't always nice. Being nice was his coworkers' jobs.

Burt saw the two bird men come in, the door emitting a soft, automated chime as they did. "Morning," he said, then saw the look on Blue's face. "Looks like you're having a shit day. Sorry, bud."

Blue's crest feathers ruffled slightly. "How...?"

"He just does that," Fuloos said. Truthfully, Fuloos liked Burt's straightforward, no-nonsense attitude. It was a nice change of pace from the usual he experienced in Seabank.

Fuloos raised a finger. "I'll take a Fudge Cookie cappuccino, medium, with extra chocolate shavings on the whipped cream." He turned to Blue. "And you?"

Blue stared at him. "Quite the sweet beak ya' got there."

Fuloos shrugged with a smile.

Blue asked Burt, "I've not been here before. What do you recommend?"

"For you?" said Burt. "You look like you've had enough bitter. Do you want something sweet or smooth?"

"Smooth."

Burt nodded. "One Blondie and a Fudge Cookie, extra sweet." He didn't tap anything to the register screen but said simply, "8 oh-5 if that's all."

Blue marveled at Burt's ability while Fuloos took care of the purchase. In an effort to not stare at the dog man too long, Blue let his falcon eyes roam throughout the store. He beheld the minimalistic decor, but had been surprised to see that he and Fuloos were the only customers in the shop currently.

"...Is it always this quiet?" he asked Burt after he finished out the register.

Burt didn't look up while he turned to the bean grinders behind him. "You made it in before lunch rush," he said simply. "Of course it's quiet. Enjoy it while you can."

Fuloos asked, "Do you have anyone coming in before lunch?"

Burt snapped the lid shut over the grinding machine. "Gurthi was supposed to be here ten minutes ago. She's always late - "

The door chime went off, and a chubby, scaly lizard girl came in, wearing a green beanie over her head and at least three layers of shirts - a cardigan, a button down, and a t-shirt. Her blue-green scales almost looked iridescent under the bare bulb light of the shop. "Sorry I'm late, boss," she said, her voice chipper but sounding out of breath.

Without looking up from his work, Burt said aloud, "Donuts are done. Go prep sandwiches and cut the cakes."

She gave a salute. "You got it, boss." And she scurried through the swinging door by the counter and disappeared into the back room.

After a moment, as the brewing machine revved to life, all three men heard Gurthie shout from the back room, "HEY BOSS, WHEN'S MARTHA COMING IN?"

Burt shouted over the machine's whirring, "SHE'LL BE HERE IN FIFTEEN."

"THAT'S CUTTIN' IT CLOSE, BOSS."

The machine ended its turn. Burt took the cup from under the drip spout. As he prepared one of the two drinks, he said, "She had to take the kids to soccer. She's coming over right after."

Gurthie poked her head out from around the corner of the back room. "Need me to call Sam?"

Burt set down a pitcher of cream and mused on the request. "...Better call Sam. They can use the extra shift, and that way Martha can take her time."

"You got it, boss." And Gurthie disappeared again.

The bell chimed as the door swung open once again. In walked a person Blue had never seen before except in movies - a rabbit person wearing a leather coat decorated in deep blue beadwork and seashells. A Lepus Lin Rabbithop. The man had yellow-brown fur and piercings up one long ear. Both ears stood straight up from his head. He looked as if he had been in the store before, tucking his hands into his coat pockets, letting his large brown eyes rest on the counter.

Once again the bells chimed with the door, and in walked a hawk man with bright green eyes, wearing the same sort of coat the rabbit man wore. The hawk man said something in a language Blue didn't understand. The rabbit man turned to him and replied back in the same language, saying something that made the hawk man chuckle.

Fuloos waved at them both and spoke in the same language. The rabbit and the hawk perked up, seeming to recognize Fuloos. The rabbit and the hawk walked up and gave fist bumps while they still spoke in that language Blue never heard before.

Eventually, Fuloos interrupted Blue's gawking by looking at him and switching back to something he knew. "Blue, this is Ylas," he gestured to the rabbit man, "and this is Havith," he gestured to the hawk. "Ylas, Havith, this is Blue."

Blue nodded at them both, unsure whether to offer a handshake or to do the first bump he saw Fuloos do. "Nice to meet you."

"Ya sure?" Ylas asked. He held up a fist. "Here's how we do it."

Taking the invitation, Blue gave him a fist bump. It made Ylas smile. "Yeah, you got it," said the rabbit man. Then Havith and Blue did the fist bump.

As they did so, Burt turned towards the back of the shop and yelled, "Gurthie! The Earth Church folks are here!"

Ylas said to Blue, "You don't look like you're from around here, brother. Where's home for you?"

Blue, startled at the friendliness of such a rough-looking rabbit folk, said, "Uh, Inlai."

Havith gave a whistle. "That far? What brings you here to Fwishi'shi?"

If Havith had called the town "Seabank," Blue would have brought his thoughts back to Roisin. But he never heard "Fwishi'shi" before, and never heard the town be referred to by any other name. He craned his head back, eyes wide and crest feathers rising in confusion. "Who? What?"

Ylas turned to his partner. "You said that on purpose."

Havith gave a shake of the head to ruffle his feathers, amused. "How often do we get to say the traditional name of the place to outsiders?"

Fuloos took a moment with Blue. "Fwishi'shi is the Rabbithop name for this town. They were the first people here."

"You," said Ylas, "and your great-grandpa. How's your house, by the way?"

"Avery and Tookis are taking a look at it. Something got in the well."

Ylas barely contained an eye roll. "Something ALWAYS gets in that well. Have you considered just...building a new one?"

Havith smacked Ylas on the arm. "New wells aren't cheap, *jufi*."

Either Ylas ignored his friend, or accepted the feedback, because he said, "Fuloos, we can do a fundraiser at the church. Your house is the last traditional dwelling in this place. We can help if you wanna keep it going."

Fuloos gave a polite smile. "I'll keep that in mind."

Before the conversation could continue, Gurthie swung through the employee-only door set in the counter, carrying two large grocery bags full of baked goods. She sang a little victory tune before passing the bags off to Ylas and Havith. The two men took the bags, and she said, "I've got two more in the back, just one sec." And she scampered off.

Blue had to ask. "What's in the bags?"

"Stuff," said Ylas.

Havith gave the more productive response. "We collect day-old baked goods from shops like this one so we can feed the kids and elders at the church. And anybody else who needs them."

Confused, Blue asked, "You go to church?" It was his impression that Rabbithops folk and other Indigenous people regarded organized church with disdain. Historically the traditional ways and the organized churches clashed more than collaborated.

"The Earth Church," Ylas corrected Blue gently. "It's run by other Rabbitfolk like us so we can keep the *ilithia jili.*"

"That's 'the tradition,'" said Havith. "...Kind of. Our language is more art than Common."

Gurthie emerged with two more bags. "Here's the last of them!" She passed one bag each to Ylas and Havith. Once both men had their hands full, Gurthie asked, "Need me to get the door?"

"Please," said Havith.

So Gurthie scurried to the main entrance and opened the door, causing the chime to go off. Havith exited first. Ylas got to the entryway, turned towards Fuloos and Blue, and said, "Fuloos, you coming tomorrow?"

"I have my radio show, remember?" Fuloos said.

"Right, forgot about that. I don't really catch the radio that often. What about Saturday?"

"Maybe Saturday."

"Give us a well update when you can, ok? The offer stands. I mean, we gotta' talk to the elders, but I'm sure they'd be willing."

Fuloos waved farewell as Ylas exited. Gurthie let the door close on its own while she hurried back to behind the counter.

Burt set two drinks on the end of the counter. "One Blondie and One Fudge Cookie."

*

The two bird men got their drinks and their seats in the Coffee Haus just before the first wave of customers came in.

Blue watched the crowd, marveling at the bustling coffee house workers. "How did this get so busy?"

"We're right by the train station," said Fuloos right before sipping his coffee. A little whipped cream got left on his beak. "And we're downtown."

Amused, Blue pointed at his own beak. "You got a little..." he gestured.

Fuloos wiped the whipped cream off with one finger, looked at it, then licked it. It made Blue snort a small chuckle.

While the crowd bustled, the drinks flowed, and the workers danced around each other to prepare orders, Fuloos asked Blue, "How are you doing right now?"

Blue took the question in, and figured that the cordial answer wouldn't do for this birdman. Blue sighed and took a sip of his coffee. It tasted smooth and warm, not a trace of bitter coffee in it, yet he could feel the positive jolt. "Just..." he said. The coffee had offset the downward spiral. "I dunno. Wondering what I did wrong?"

Fuloos asked him, "You're a photographer by trade, right?"

At this, Blue nodded.

"Do you like your work?"

He hadn't really thought about that for a while. He gave a tilt of the head. Over the din of the coffee grinder doing its job, he said, "...I like the assignments I get that resonate with me."

"And what resonates?"

"...Remember when I was here a few months ago? I was here for an assignment with Wings of Peace. That meant a lot to me."

"Oh?"

"I mean, my parents are Blue Little-feathers who adopted me. My birth parents didn't like that I was...uh..." he tapped the tip of his cane to the floor.

At this, Fuloos noted the cane and said, "So that's been a constant?"

Blue nodded. "It doesn't bother me much," he said. "But it makes me feel like I can't keep up with...anybody."

"...Is that why you work so hard?"

At this, Blue blinked and turned his head to the older birdman.

Fuloos sipped his drink. "Roisin mentioned you work long hours."

"I do. But..." He gazed down at the coffee in his mug. "I hadn't really thought about it like that before."

"But you work hard, right?"

"...I do."

"And why's that?"

"To get paid so I can get nice things for Roisin and me." Blue set his cup down. "I like getting gifts and giving them. It's just..."

"Just what?"

Blue leaned forward in his seat. "It's not that I get presents to avoid the other person or something. I just like giving things. I like finding something that someone's gonna like and seeing the look on their face when they get it. It makes me happy when I find and give something that makes the other person happy."

Something twinkled in Fuloos's eyes. "...What's a gift that stands out to you? What was your favorite one to give so far?"

Blue really had to think on that one. He whistled in thought, leaning an elbow on the table and holding his cheek. There was the time he got Stacy a rare Pajammers band T-shirt he found at a thrift store in downtown Inlai. There was the time he got Raheem lunch when the human had a very bad day. Or when he got foam swords with his old college roommate and they both fake-sword fought down their halls.

Then he remembered a gift that didn't cost him much but meant a lot.

"...That time Roisin and I sat in on a radio interview you did."

"Oh don't flatter me like that - "

"No, I'm serious!" Blue sat up. "You didn't see how excited she was to listen in. She could barely sit still next to me, she was so giddy." Blue thought back on that memory and smiled. "It made me happy to see her happy."

Fuloos smiled and sipped his drink. By this point the both of them were getting to the bottoms of their cups.

Blue realized that Fuloos had gotten Blue to talk about himself - but the same could not be said for the other way around. He wanted to tip the scale of the conversation a little to make it more even. So Blue asked, "Have you ever been in love?"

Fuloos froze. He had been ready to set his mug down, and now it hovered mere inches above the table. Blue could see the other man's finger tips tighten ever so slightly.

"...Once," said Fuloos.

Blue's crest feathers bristled. "I didn't mean to upset you - "

"You didn't," Fuloos said. His own feathers hadn't shifted on his head, but he set his mug down and started picking a finger into his arm feathers. "I just haven't thought about her for a long time. It was years ago."

Blue regretted asking, but now he felt he had to finish what he started. "...What was she like?"

Fuloos kept his eyes lowered, gazing at his cup. One finger started tracing the rim. "...How familiar are you with sea nymphs?"

Blue didn't know where Fuloos was going with this question. Did the red-feathered man actually hook up with one? Blue answered, "...Not very. I just know they occupy the sea in places mermaids don't live."

Fuloos gave a small smirk. "You're not wrong. Mermaids live much further out to sea, beyond the shelf. Sea nymphs live where the water and the shore meet." His finger stopped tracing the cup's rim. "...One used to live on the beach here in Seabank."

"Really?"

"Sea nymphs live a long time. Longer than elves, even." Which was saying something. Blue recalled seeing in the news that the oldest elf currently alive was somewhere to the tune of 240 years old. And sea nymphs lived longer than that?

Fuloos continued, unaware of Blue's thoughts. "You may not be aware, but my house - my ancestral home - is built into the cliff right next to the sea. My great-grandfather carved it out of the rocks."

"...Woah."

"He told his grandson - my father - that he settled there because he heard the sea whisper to him. The whispers, he discovered, came from the sea nymph who lived there since the days the Buteo Ja and Lepus Lin started living here." Upon seeing Blue's confused face, Fuloos clarified, "...The Buteo Ja and Lepus Lin are the hawks and rabbits who make up the Rabbithops people."

"Wait, so...your great-grandpa met a sea nymph THAT old?"

"She was dying at the time, and asked my great-grandfather to watch over the sea until a new sea nymph could settle there. He respected her wishes and kept the family there. A new nymph didn't come by until I was about..." Fuloos raised his eyes in thought, as if trying to conjure the memory in his mind. "...I think I was twelve."

Blue blinked and ruffled his head feathers. "Twelve?"

"When I first saw her, she looked like she was my age. But it's hard to tell with sea nymphs. They don't age the same way everyone else does. But I only saw her a handful of times before I left for school as a young man." Fuloos lifted his cup, keeping one elbow on the table so he could look into it. Only whipped cream and chocolate shavings were left. "I didn't see her again until I came back and moved back into the house."

"Wait," said Blue. He didn't know of any colleges in Seabank - only a branch college in Treeta, an hour away by train. When Blue put the pieces together in his mind, he realized that Fuloos had to travel. "You moved back?"

"I couldn't leave my great-grandfather's home behind," Fuloos said. "It's a part of the history here. It should be preserved. And after the death of my parents, no one was left to care for it except me."

"Wow. That's...that's a lot. I'm sorry they're gone."

Fuloos nodded for Blue's sympathy. "It was just me in that ancient house until the sea nymph came back. She started to show herself again about a week after I returned."

"What was her name?"

At this, Fuloos chuckled. "Unpronounceable for people like us. She tried to teach me it once but I couldn't do it. So she asked me to call her Star. It was the rough translation of her name into our language." His eyes wandered, eventually settling on a spot in the far distance. His shoulders drooped, his breathing slowed. Even the din of the coffee shop seemed to quiet down. Blue didn't know what the man was thinking, but eventually Fuloos sighed. "I could have married that woman."

"...But?"

"Sea nymphs don't marry. Besides, even if they did, she wanted to raise her children in the water."

"And you didn't?"

"I'm a red-feather. We don't live in the sea." He tapped his fingers quietly on the table. "I haven't seen her for five years."

At once, a loud whistle came from outside. Even the other coffee shop customers went silent to listen.

Fuloos perked up at the whistles outside. "...Avery's back."

"Wait, what?" asked Blue.

"That was him just now." Fuloos got out of his seat, picking up his drained cup. "I asked him to take a look at my well. Sounds like he's back in town."

"You could tell that from a whistle?" Blue slowly got out of his seat, using his cane and the table to help himself up. His leg started to feel a bit better, but he didn't want to put too much strain on it.

As the din of the coffee shop resumed, Fuloos took Blue's empty cup and said, "It's Faiji - the whistling language we use here in town."

Blue made a humming sound. "No wonder you don't use cell phones. So, can I come with you?" He felt silly asking, but he didn't necessarily want to be alone. More importantly, he didn't want Fuloos to be alone, either.

Fuloos's arm feathers and crest feathers perked up a bit. "...You sure? It's likely going to be boring."

"Well, I don't know where Roisin ran off to. And I think giving her space would be the better move right now."

"Fair enough."

The whistles came from outside again. Fuloos dropped the cups off at a counter by the trash can, poked his head out the store's entrance, and whistled loudly in response. He turned to Blue and said, "I told him we're on our way. Let's go."

*

Roisin had run out of Jenny's Bookshop, utterly frustrated and angry, and above all, grieving. She hated feeling the weight of these emotions in her chest, so she rented a bike from a nearby kiosk and pedaled hard and fast to the beach. It felt as if the wind helped carry her there as it rushed against her back. She didn't see any traffic except for a pick-up truck driving away from the sea. As soon as she got to the cliff, she kicked off the bike and ran down the pass to get to the beach. And once her feet touched the sand, she slowed until she fell to her knees. She curled in on herself and hugged her arms around her.

At once, the tears fell. She let out a howl to banish the weight in her chest, hoping the sea would take her feelings and wash them out to the horizon. She hated feeling this miserable. She hated feeling this ignored. Like no matter what she said, no one would listen. That Blue wouldn't listen. And Blue was who needed to hear her the most.

So, she cried. She cried to banish the building frustration, the simmering hatred against the world that was beginning to bubble up. She rested her forehead on the sand and let the tears fall. She cried so long that the sea's tide started to wash up, brushing the tears away.

This startled her out of her grief. She remembered from reading about the sea at Seabank that high tide didn't happen at this height unless it was a full moon. And yesterday's moon was waning into the empty new phase.

She lifted her head, confused by nature's whims.

And then she saw her.

There, in the water, stood a woman. A voluptuous woman, with teal green skin and dark blue hair, long and wet and undulating in waves like the water around her concealed feet. The waves passed over her ankles and brushed against Roisin's knees. She wore a dress that, upon closer inspection, appeared to be woven out of seaweed. It clung to her figure and did not blow in the breeze the same way her hair did.

The woman gazed at Roisin with blank, blue eyes, absent of pupils or sclera. Her mouth opened, and she said, "You have been crying," with a voice as deep as a trench.

Roisin sniffed. She nodded, wiping a trail of tears off one cheek.

"I brought the sea closer to wash your tears away."

This just made Roisin cry harder.

The woman approached and knelt down in front of her. She made no move to touch Roisin, keeping her hands in her lap. She said, "Why are you crying?"

Roisin sniffed. She wanted to say so many things. That the man she loved would never understand what she desired. That she felt so alone. That all she wanted was someone to be with her, to spend time with her, the same way Fuloos did.

But all that Roisin could say was, "...It's so hard to love someone who doesn't understand you."

The woman lifted her hands and held Roisin's shoulders, pulling as if asking for permission. At this, Roisin relented and embraced the woman.

She didn't know what to expect - cold, maybe? Like hugging something wet that just came out of a pool. But the woman felt warm, like a hot spring rumbling to ease the aches away. The woman smelled like sea salt.

"I know this feeling better than you may realize," the woman said to her. "And I am sorry you are going through this."

Roisin gave the woman a squeeze and leaned back. She sniffed. The woman raised a hand and wiped the other stream of tears off her cheek. It startled her that the woman's hands felt thick and strong, like a swimmer's.

The woman asked, "What's your name?"

"...Roisin," she hiccuped. "I'm sorry you have to see me like this."

"I have seen so many people in so many ways," said the woman. "You are fine just the way you are, Roisin."

She looked into the woman's solid blue eyes. "...What's your name?" she asked to be polite.

"Your people cannot pronounce it. But you can call me Star."

"...Star?"

"That's what my true name comes out to in your language. The man who lives here also calls me Star." The woman looked around the beach. "...Where is the man who lives here? The red-feathered man?"

"...Fuloos?" Upon getting a nod from the woman, Roisin said, "He's in town. Why?"

"...I need to give him a warning."

This alarmed Roisin. "...A warning for what?"

"A storm is coming. A large one. From the sea. It's going to strike this town tonight. I fear his ancestral home will not survive. Tell Fuloos he must stay away from the sea. For his own safety."

"How do you know there's a storm coming?"

Star pointed an outstretched arm behind her. Roisin looked over her shoulder and saw - far, far away, miles away, maybe - enormous gray and black clouds rolling. The spotted gray clouds above that shielded the sun seemed friendly in comparison to this storm.

"...Oh no." Roisin couldn't stop the words from coming out.

"You must find Fuloos. Find the elders, as well. They know what to do."

"...The elders? The elders of what?"

"The elders of the first people here. I believe they're called the... Rabbithops?" Star made a face, as if the word sounded foreign. "My people call them the Buteo Ja and the Lepus Lin. The elders are in town. Find them and warn them of the storm."

"But what about you?"

Star held Roisin's hands. "I am from the sea," she said. "I know the safe places to shelter in storms like this. They're just not accessible for land dwellers." Star looked Roisin right in the eyes. Though her own were one solid color, Roisin could see a shine to them, and the pinch of the eyelids and brows that expressed her concern. "Can you do this? I cannot leave the sea. I need you to deliver this message for me. Please."

In truth, Roisin still felt the weight in her chest. She didn't feel ready to leave the beach. She didn't want to go back into town. It would mean a greater likelihood of coming across Blue - the last person she wanted to see at that moment.

But then she thought of Fuloos. She thought of him coming home without hearing the warning. She could picture a storm blowing in, tossing waves into his ancestral house, locking him in - or worse.

For him. She would do this for him. Fuloos was a kind man. And Roisin didn't want him hurt.

Roisin nodded to the woman. "...Ok." She wiped her face to get the tears and sand off. "Ok, I'll go into town. I would use that whistling language, but I don't know it. So I'll go back."

"Do so quickly," Star implored. She stole a glance over her shoulder. The storm clouds had moved in closer - alarmingly closer. "At this speed, it will be here by nightfall."

"Then I better get going." Roisin got to her feet, helping Star get to hers. "You should hide while you can."

"I will see you off first." Star touched her forehead to Roisin's. "Be safe, Roisin."

"You too, Star." Roisin let the feeling of the hot spring touch her head. Then she stepped away and ran up the pass.

*

"...Unsalvageable?"

Avery nodded sadly. "Tookis took a closer look at it to be sure."

Tookis - Avery's brother who inherited the height and weight Avery lacked, said in a deep voice, "Part of the pipes broke off and fell in, bringing some of the rock in with it. Neither of us can reach it, it's too deep. And whatever knocked that pipe loose - " His monkey nose wrinkled. "It STANK."

"Stank something AWFUL," Avery confirmed. "Pretty sure something got into the pipe and died, and then the pressure built up behind it and PWISH - " he gestured to show an explosion.

Fuloos took off his glasses and pinched the space above his beak, his eyes squeezing shut. He didn't know what to expect, but he didn't expect this.

Blue patted Fuloos on the shoulder. "I'm sorry, man. That sounds rough."

Fuloos nodded. "It means we'll have to either get the right tools to dig it out, or close the well off."

"I would close it off," said Avery. "That well was looking pretty low when we took a closer look."

"Not to bring up a sore point," said Blue, "but remember when Ylas and Havith mentioned they could help?"

"Oh?" Avery and Tookis both said in unison.

Fuloos sighed, letting go of his face. "We can talk about that later -
"

A loud whistle came from further in town. A warning whistle, one Fuloos hadn't heard in a long time. And apparently, judging by the shocked looks on the brothers' faces, neither had Avery or Tookis.

Blue tilted his head in confusion. "What was that?" he asked.

Avery said, "The Elders of the Earth Church. They just announced a storm's coming."

Tookis turned towards the sea, shielding his eyes to focus better on the horizon. "Oh cripes," he said. "That's a biggin' comin' in, too. Biggest one I've ever seen."

Avery climbed onto Tookis' back - being small and nimble, he could do so easily - and peered into the horizon. Something moved in the corner of his vision, so he turned to spot whatever he saw. "Hey," he slapped Tookis' shoulder. "It's that red-head we saw hoofing it to the shore. She's coming back into town."

Blue perked up at the description of "red-head." "Is she wearing a dress? A blue dress?"

Avery narrowed his eyes to peer closer. "Yup. Blue and white. She's riding towards the center of town. Towards Jenny's."

"That's Roisin!"

Fuloos' brows furrowed. "Why towards Jenny's? Because that's where we last saw her?"

"Well whatever the reason," Avery said, still peering into the distance, "she's talking to Ingrid." He glanced down at his brother. "Ingrid knows Faiji, right?"

Tookis nodded. "Yup."

"Ok, so she heard the signal." Avery peered back out to the distance. "Op. Looks like your girlfriend's hiking it towards the Earth Church." He turned back to Fuloos and Blue with a fanged monkey smile. His furry tail twitched. "Need a ride there?"

*

Roisin stopped to speak with Ingrid to get directions to the Elders. Ingrid told her to go straight to the Earth Church, down Market Street - or was it Mark Street? No, Market. Roisin saw the sign and took the turn on her bike. She had asked Ingrid if she would be alright, to which the woman replied, "We'll be fine. Just go there, and then go straight home. Or wherever you're staying, I know you're not local."

It made Roisin start to worry about the others she had met in town. Misses Ridgeway in her bed and breakfast. Ingrid in her shop. Pat - there was Pat, driving her car towards the Earth Church. She slowed the car down to keep pace with Roisin's bike. "You heard the warning signal?" the cat woman asked.

Roisin nodded. "Yes. I have to get to the elders."

"Park that bike. I can get you there faster."

Roisin dropped the bike off at a bike rack in front of the bike rental shop, then jumped into the passenger seat of Pat's car. The two sped off until they got to the Earth Church.

The Earth Church - to Roisin's surprise - didn't look like any church she knew. The ones she knew had been large, multi-story affairs, the kinds of venues that occupied former strip malls or shopping malls and slapped their icons on the windows. But the Earth Church here? It looked like a dome. A dome the size of Jenny's Bookstore and just as wide. Strange symbols had been painted and carved on the dome in places where grass did not grow. Towards the top of the dome grew small sapling trees.

Pat parked the car. "The elders should be inside," she said to Roisin.

Roisin turned to her, unbuckling her seat belt. "Have you seen Fuloos?"

Pat shook her head. "Sorry. Not today."

"If you find him, tell him I have to talk to him right away." And Roisin got out of the car.

Pat shouted after her, "Are you going to still be here?!"

Roisin did not answer. She just ran to the church's entrance.

A rabbit man stepped out, piercings running up one of his long ears, wearing a leather jacket covered in turquoise and sea shells. He spotted Roisin and asked, "Woah, what's the rush?"

"I heard the whistle," she said. "Do the elders know about the - "

"The storm?" As if on cue, they heard thunder in the far distance. "Yeah. Heviithi spotted it about half an hour ago."

"Have you seen Fuloos?" Roisin asked.

The rabbit man smiled. "Yeah! Last I saw him, he was at the Coffee Haus. Him and uh..." he snapped his fingers. "...his name was a color, I think - "

"Blue?"

"Yeah! Blue!"

"But Fuloos is at the Coffee Haus?"

The rabbit man spotted something over Roisin's shoulder. And then the both of them could hear an engine running. Roisin turned around and saw an old pick-up truck - the same one she had passed earlier when she had been riding towards the beach. She could see Fuloos and a large monkey man in the truck bed, Fuloos looking ready to jump out of the back as soon as the vehicle would stop. And there, in the passenger's seat, Blue, holding on to the grip above the door, next to a smaller monkey man driving the truck.

Fuloos jumped out before the truck could come to a full stop. He dashed up to Roisin and the rabbit man. "Roisin!"

"Fuloos!" Roisin ran to him and tackled him in a hug. Fuloos's arms wrapped around her. He wasn't as warm as the woman from the sea, but his presence felt just as reassuring.

She took a step back - not seeing the pained expression on Blue's face after he came slowly out of the truck. She said to Fuloos, "I have to tell you - you have to stay in town. Don't go back home."

"Wait, what?" Fuloos stared at her.

"The storm. It's coming in, and it's gonna' be big. So big it could wreck your house."

The rabbit man behind her said, "Oh shit." She heard his steps retreating quickly behind her.

Fuloos shook his head. "No. No, that house will be fine. It's survived storms before - "

"LISTEN TO ME," Roisin held his shoulders. It frightened him enough to snap his beak shut and stare at her, wide-eyed. She didn't want to yell, but she was sick and tired of being ignored. "DO. NOT. GO. BACK. HOME." She spoke slowly to drive it home. "The storm will hit your house. The sea nymph told me so."

Roisin had never seen color drain out of a birdman's face until she saw Fuloos in front of her. He said nothing at first.

Blue approached from the side. "...The sea nymph?" he asked. Roisin expected him to disbelieve her, but to her surprise, he said, "You saw her?"

Roisin nodded. "She said her name was Star. She came out of the sea and told me," she looked at Fuloos, "to tell you - DO NOT GO HOME."

She saw a million thoughts race behind Fuloos' eyes all at once. He held her hands, the ones holding his shoulders - and him - in place. He took those hands in his own, and lowered them. And he said to Roisin, "I have to go."

He turned at once and ran to the pick-up truck.

Roisin felt ready to slap him, "YOU'RE NOT - " she screamed.

Blue held her back. She spun on him, ready to yell at him, as well, the rage bubbling -

And as soon as she saw his eyes, that rage fizzled out. Blue's falcon eyes implored her to stop. "It's not just the house," he said to her quietly. "...It's not just the house."

Roisin watched as the pick-up truck carried the two monkey men - and Fuloos - away, towards the beach. She sighed, her shoulders slumping down as the truck turned and vanished out of sight.

She could hear bustling behind her. She could hear Blue talking to the rabbit man - Ylas, she discovered when Blue said his name. "What do we do?"

"Havith is getting the team together. We're gonna' go to his house and pack up as much as we can before the storm hits."

"What about the rest of the town?"

"They're getting ready as best as they can. If you need to, the church's basement doubles as a shelter. We have some out-of-towners down there already."

Roisin's hand moved on its own and grabbed Blue by the shirt collar. Blue held still, but turned his gaze ever so slowly towards her, frightened.

She looked him in the eyes and said to him, "...Please go to Misses Ridgeway. She needs help."

Blue's crest feathers went straight up, his pupils dilated. "What are you planning?"

"I have to go after Fuloos before he does something stupid." She wriggled out of his grasp and ran towards Pat's car.

Blue shouted her name but she ignored him. She got into the passenger's seat - two other people were shifting into the seats in the back. Roisin asked, "Can you get me to the beach?"

"After I drop these people off," said Pat. "Their destination is halfway. Why? The storm's coming quickly."

"I need to get to Fuloos."

*

The pick-up truck bumped and rumbled across the dirt road to the cliff. The thunder rumbled - closer this time - the daylight vanishing behind deep gray clouds. As the truck rolled quickly down, Tookis sat in the truck bed with Fuloos. The bird man kept his sharp eyes on the cliff and nothing else. He didn't even seem to notice the misting rain that began to fall and turn the shoulders of both men misty damp.

Tookis heard the whistle from town. The elders were sending young people to the cliff house. Maybe to shore up the place? Keep it safe from the storm? Tookis whistled back that he and Avery were with Fuloos.

Avery parked the truck at the bike shelter on the top of the cliff. Fuloos was jumping off before the vehicle came to a complete halt. Fuloos ran right for the pass, ignoring Avery yelling after him.

This made the smaller monkey man turn to his bigger brother. "He's lost his mind," he said.

"Nevermind that," said Tookis. "Get on the platform. I'll lower you down. Start loading it up with anything that looks important."

"We're not sandbagging this?"

The thunder rumbled overhead. The sea waves crashed louder below.

"No," said Tookis. "We are not."

*

Fuloos' feet kept sliding underneath him as he ran down the sandy Oloos Pass. He could smell the salt and the alkaline in the air intensify as the thunder rumbled louder and closer than ever. He didn't care.

Where was Star?

As soon as he hit the bottom of the cliff, he pulled his shoes off. Then his vest and shirt, tossing them aside. Of course the rain decided to come down from a mist to a steady drizzle. His body felt the rain hit him, but his mind kept to one thing.

Why hadn't she made herself known up until now? Why talk to Roisin? Was it because he wasn't there? Did she hate him now? He didn't understand - he thought their split was mutually agreed upon. That they couldn't stay together - he a man of the beach and she a woman of the sea.

The water's waves rose higher, crashing closer and closer to the edges of his home. He ran out into the water.

"STAR!"

Only the waves rushing at his legs. He called for her again.

The thunder roared.

Something flashed in the distance. Lightning.

He had to find her. He took a deep breath - before a wave struck him in the chest - and he dove into the water.

*

Roisin leaped out of the car before Pat could even park it. She saw the larger of the monkey men on the cliff. "Excuse me!" she called him.

The man turned to her. "Oh. Name's Tookis. You are?" He started pulling rope to haul something.

"Roisin. Where's Fuloos?"

"Down below." A platform appeared on the other end of the rope, loaded with a suitcase and a box full of pantry staples and a very old cookbook Roisin recognized. Tookis wrapped the rope's end in place and began to unload the platform.

Roisin took a peek over the edge of the cliff. She saw Fuloos rip his vest and shirt off and start running towards the water.

"FULOOS!" she screamed. But he didn't hear her. The rain came down harder than before.

Tookis said, "He's been ignoring everybody. Can ya' help us load up the truck?"

Roisin turned to him. "Lower me down on the platform. Please."

His fur stood on end and bristled around the edges of his shirt. "WHAT?"

"This thing can hold the weight of a person, right? If it can, lower me down. I need to get to him."

"But what can - "

"I'm a certified lifeguard. If he tries to go out to sea, I can catch him."

They both heard Fuloos scream from the waves for Star. But only the thunder roared above.

Tookis' nostrils flared as he stared at Roisin. "...Get on the platform. I'll get you down."

Roisin got on - causing the thing to rock for a moment - but Tookis got to lowering her down immediately. They could both hear Avery screaming from the rock house at Fuloos. Halfway down the cliff, Roisin saw Fuloos dive under the water. She jumped off the platform before it could touch the ground and started running to the sea.

"Wait a minute!" Avery shouted at her, but she ignored him.

Tookis could barely register a series of vehicles pulling up behind him. He shouted at Avery from the top of the cliff, "Keep going! She's a lifeguard!"

"But even a lifeguard will have trouble with these waves!"

"Then hurry up before they get worse and you get caught in them!"

*

Fuloos dove down into the waves and immediately regretted it. He felt the cold sink under his feathers, under his skin. He thought if he didn't keep swimming, the cold would make his muscles seize.

He saw no sign of Star. Only fish retreating to a space beyond. Even the starfish and shellfish dug themselves under the sand.

He felt the tide hit him in the chest, knocking the breath out of him. He fought the urge to gasp for air. Not here. Not under the water.

He powered through and kept swimming. She had to be here.

Then he saw eyes, and he froze.

Those eyes did not belong to Star. They were angry. Full of wrath.

Something sped through the tides and struck him in the chest. Without meaning to, he gasped, and water came rushing into his lungs. He felt heavy. His chest felt heavy. He stopped struggling - everything in him slowed down.

And then he felt something grab him from behind and pull him away. Just before he blacked out, he saw those vicious eyes once more before the thing that hit him swam back into the abyss.

*

Roisin pulled Fuloos' limp body onto the sand. She grunted and kept dragging him away from the water so the waves wouldn't wash them both out. She kept her panic down as best she could - she had seen him take in a gulp of water when the electric eel struck him in the chest.

To earth. She had to drag him to earth first, before anything else.

Roisin pulled Fuloos close to the cliff edge - just before reaching the bucket chain of people of all walks and builds stacking things onto the platform. One of the bucket chain members - Pat - saw Fuloos and Roisin, and panicked. "Fuloos!" She started to run -

"Stay there!" Roisin shouted at her. "I got this! I can resuscitate him!"

Ylas shouted from the cave, "Pat! Get back in line! We gotta hurry!"

Pat gave a curt nod to Roisin and hurried back.

Roisin, however, did not feel as confident. She got him out of the water - she was glad she still had the strength to do that. It had been too long since she acted as a lifeguard. But she never had to resuscitate a drowning victim. Of course she practiced on a variety of dummies, from human to bird men. But could she remember how to do this in her panic?

She started by pressing her ear to his chest, hoping for a heart beat.

She felt a faint, weak pulse. Good. He wasn't beyond saving.

She clasped her hands and started pushing on his chest in the rhythm she had practiced so many times on so many dummies. She counted each push until she reached ten.

Roisin tilted his head back.

To her shock, she didn't have to do anything else - Fuloos coughed up water and rolled onto his side, hacking until he began to wheeze for breath.

She let out the breath she didn't even know she was holding. "Oh thank the gods," she sighed.

Fuloos tried to prop himself up on his shaking arms. Roisin held him around the middle and said, "Fuloos, you nearly drowned. We're taking you back to town. Now."

He gazed up at her, dazed. "...Roisin?"

"Yes," she said. "Yes, it's me."

He winced at something - a pang in his chest maybe. He had been struck by an electric eel. There may have still been a stinger in his system.

Roisin let go of him slowly. "Let me get a good look at you," she said, rolling him onto his back. She let her eyes drift down his surprisingly lean figure and -

Yep. There on his belly. Small, but sharp. She held it and said to him, "I'm pulling this out on the count of three. Ready?"

He gave a nod.

"Onetwothree!" She pulled.

A sharp squawk came out of him and he doubled over in pain. Roisin threw the barb back into the sea's waves - which were now beginning to lap at their feet. The thunder cracked overhead - directly overhead. The rain, which Roisin didn't notice until now, drenched them just as much as the ocean did.

"Okay!" shouted Ylas, who - like the other members of the bucket chain - wore a bright yellow poncho with the hood pulled over his head. "That's the most important stuff! We gotta go!"

Avery shouted from the house's entrance, "But there's still things in here!"

"We can't get it all! We gotta go before the waves hit us!"

Roisin held her hands on Fuloos' bare shoulders. She cupped one hand on his cheek to make him look her in the eyes.

"Is there anything super important in that house you absolutely need?"

She could see his thoughts swimming - she hated asking him to pick the most important possessions after he just survived near-death.

Fuloos turned to the closest member of the bucket chain - Pat. "Did you get the tea kettle?"

She nodded.

"And my mother's cookbook?"

"Yes."

Avery shouted from the house, "It was the first thing I packed!"

Fuloos gave a weak nod. "That's all I need."

Roisin lifted one of his arms around her shoulder. "Ok. Let's go."

Pat darted to his other side and did the same. "Let's get him on the platform. He's in no condition to go up the pass."

Ylas shouted at the rest of the brigade, "Alright! That's all she wrote, folks! Let's get outta' here!"

Roisin and Pat carried Fuloos' weak body to the platform as the bright yellow brigade ran past them and up Oloos Pass, with the remaining belongings in tow. The platform already had three things on there, so it only had weight left for Fuloos and Roisin. Pat helped them on and, as soon as Tookis and Havith pulled on the rope from the top, she ran up the pass faster than the others.

The platform itself scared Roisin in that moment, more than possibly drowning in the waters below. The sea waves crashed against the cliff now - so hard that the splash backs touched the bottom of the platform while it rocked with motion. She tried to keep her eyes on the rope of the pulley system so she wouldn't think of the ocean trying to swallow them again. But the aging gears and rope didn't help at all. Neither did the rain falling hard and fast - so much that she could barely see anything beyond three feet in front of her.

Fuloos laced his fingers between hers and held it tight. And with his other arm he pulled her into a hug. A tight one. Which she reciprocated.

"...Thank you," he said in her ear over the din of the storm.

*

The brigade drove their two pickup trucks and a van off towards the Earth Church. The boxes filled the trucks, leaving the van to hold the bright yellow bucket brigade members, drenched but proud. Tookis and Avery drove to the Cuddly Nook, per Roisin's request. Pat got back in her car and followed Tookis and Avery's pickup closely. Fuloos had been laid across her back seats.

As soon as Tookis parked the truck, Blue opened the front door of the Cuddly Nook. He saw Roisin come out first and hurry to Pat's car. Avery came out close behind and said to Blue, "Keep that door propped open, buddy!"

So Blue angled himself to keep his back on the door to hold it open wide. He shouted to the inside, "Roisin's back!"

The aforementioned Roisin and Pat pulled Fuloos out of the car, just in time for Tookis to scoop the bird man up with his thick, hairy arms like a parent carrying a sick child. Pat turned to Blue. "Is Doctor Ruma in?"

Blue turned his head back to the inside of the house. "Is there a Doctor Ruma in?" he called. A shout from the house gave the affirmative. Blue turned back. "Get him on the couch. Quick."

Tookis bowed his head under the porch's roof as well as the door jamb, turning himself sideways to fit through. It was a tight squeeze, even if Blue hadn't been there to hold open the door.

Avery said, "Pat, help me get some of these boxes into the basement before they get soaked." He would have asked Roisin to help, but the human woman had run after Tookis carrying Fuloos.

As soon as she crossed the threshold, Blue reached out and held her hand. "Roisin, what happened?" he asked, worried.

"He tried jumping into the ocean and an electric eel stung him in the chest," she said.

"Holy shit," his eyes widened.

"Outta' the way!" shouted Avery as he approached the door, pulling a wheeled suitcase with one hand and carrying a box with the other. Roisin stepped up on the stairs to get out of Avery's way. The monkey man took a look at Blue and said, "You can either keep holding the door or help us unload. We gotta' pull some stuff in."

Thunder boomed directly overhead. The lights in the house flickered.

Avery and Pat hurried off to the other side of the living room.

Roisin took one look at Blue. "Can you carry things?"

"I'll just hold the door. Storm's making my leg hurt worse."

"Do you need to sit down?"

"Nah. This'll keep my foot from going numb." He gave a nod to the truck outside. "You should go help them carry stuff in, though, before the storm REALLY hits."

Roisin stepped down from the stairs but then Blue said, "Wait a minute." He took a step around the door to something out of sight, then came back with a thick raincoat. "Better wear this."

She took it. "Thanks," she said, slipping it on.

"You said he jumped in the ocean, right?"

"Mmhmm." She zipped the coat shut. "I had to pull him out of the sea."

"Cuz' you're a badass," he said, smiling.

To her own surprise, she smiled back at him. "I didn't feel badass in the moment," she admitted. "But I suppose I was." She took a step up to him and gave him a quick kiss on the cheek. "I'll be right back."

As she left out the door and hopped down the porch steps, Blue shouted after her, "You smell like seaweed!"

She flipped him off before climbing into the back of the pick-up truck. He smiled - the Roisin he knew was back.

*

The elderly Doctor Ruma - the wrinkled Basset hound dog man who usually spent his time smoking his pipe on the porch - now held his pipe away from Fuloos as he pressed a floppy ear to the birdman's chest. Every once in a while, Fuloos would try to say something to Avery as the monkey man passed by with a box full of belongings. This would prompt the old dog man to give a warning woof and narrow his wrinkled eyes. And that, in turn, would make Fuloos sink into his seat on the couch, silent.

Tookis would pause the box unloading and watch the proceedings carefully. Then he would return to the box brigade.

Thankfully the truck didn't take very long to unload, and once that had been done, the Makekis brothers sat in separate chairs in the living room, waiting for Doctor Ruma to finish checking over Fuloos. Roisin had run upstairs to get out of her wet clothes and into something dry - baggy pajama pants and a cropped tank top, with a shawl pulled around her shoulders. Pat helped Misses Ridgeway in the kitchen prepare soup and tea for the guests.

Soon, on the opposite side of the house, Blue and Roisin whispered among themselves - Roisin to catch him up on what happened at the cliff, and Blue to catch her up on who Star was exactly and what she had meant to their older friend.

"Oh my gods," Roisin gasped once everything had been shared.

"I know," Blue said quietly. "...I still can't believe a sea nymph actually talked to you."

"Right?" She couldn't believe it either - as wild as their world was, sea nymphs were practically legendary.

"Cuz' you're a badass," Blue said, smiling at her.

Roisin gave him a nudge in the shoulder. But she was smiling, too. They let a small silence fall over them while the two cat women cooked in the kitchen. They could both hear the rain on the roof, even two and a half stories above them. The thunder rumbled - not overhead this time, but still close to the house. They both heard one of the cat women hiss at the storm.

Blue broke the silence first. "I don't wanna' leave yet."

Roisin looked at him. "...What?"

"I don't wanna' leave Seabank yet," he said to her. "I'm worried about Fuloos." He didn't even say 'I'm worried about us.' "I wanna' make sure he's gonna' be alright."

"But," Roisin said, "you got here by train, right? Don't you have a return trip?"

He shook his head. "I took a one-way, not a round-trip. Like, Joel told me - " he paused, his eyes widened. "Oh shit you weren't supposed to know that."

"Goddammit, Joel," said Roisin, folding her arms across her chest. But her irritation didn't last long. "So they told you I was here?"

"Yeah," Blue confessed, a little sheepish. "They told me the date of your return trip, but I figured you - we - would be leaving on a different day. And uh," he scratched the back of his feathery head, "Round-trip tickets were absolutely bananas to get at the last-minute. It was a little easier to get stuff together for a one-way. And then we would...figure out the rest from there."

Roisin stared at him in awe. "That's...unusually open-ended for you."

He shrugged, a small smile on his beak. He took a step towards her - and she towards him. And then he pulled her in for a hug. And she wrapped her arms around him.

"I'm glad you're still around," he said to her.

She nodded into his chest. "It was absolutely terrifying out there," she said. "I'm glad to be back, too."

The pair let go and took a good, long look into each others' eyes. And Blue said, "Don't worry about us right now. We'll figure that out later - "

Almost on cue, Misses Ridgeway called in a sing-song from the kitchen, "Soup's ready!"

Roisin took a look towards the kitchen and then back to Blue. "...Yeah." She smiled. "Yeah. We'll figure that out later. Let's make sure Fuloos is ok."

*

Roisin helped Misses Ridgeway and Pat pass around bowls of steamy noodle soup with buttery bread rolls to everyone in the living room. Doctor Ruma kept his on the coffee table and sat back on the edge of it, giving Fuloos a quick look-over. "You said you were struck by an electric eel?"

As Fuloos nodded, Roisin said, "I pulled the barb out of his chest. Just above his belly button."

Ruma's old eyes drooped down to the spot in question. He gave a harumph. "I wouldn't have noticed unless you said something. Very clean. Good job."

Fuloos winced. "It still hurts when I breathe."

Roisin gasped. "Oh no - did I accidentally break your ribs? I had to do CPR - "

Fuloos shook his head. "No," he groaned. "I've broken my ribs before. This isn't like that."

Blue's brows furrowed over his sharp eyes. "Wait, when did you - "

"College," said Fuloos. "Let me tell you, that HURT like a motherfucker." Then he realized the company in the room and turned to Misses Ridgeway, the elderly cat woman with thick glasses. "Sorry, Misses Ridgeway - "

She waved it off. "Oh, don't you worry about it," she said. "I founded the EMT squad in this community, and let me tell you, in the decades I ran in the back of the E-squad, I have heard more colorful language than that." She gave a knowing smile. "Ever see bone sticking out of skin? THAT'S a cause for speaking in tongues."

Some in the room winced while Avery, grinning, said, "Gnarly."

Misses Ridgeway lowered her head to peer at Fuloos over the rims of her thick glasses. "Now, you're probably tired because you drowned, sweetie. That'll make anybody tired. You be sure to give Roisin your gratitude for pulling your silly butt out of the water."

"Yes, ma'am," Fuloos gave a sheepish nod.

"Now let me go find you a change of clothes - "

"I got it," Avery got out of his seat. "I packed that suitcase for him with some dirty laundry I found in a pile. Figured if it's dirty, that means you wear it often."

As Avery passed to the staircase to climb to the second floor, Fuloos thought on his wisdom. "...You're not wrong."

Over time, Fuloos acquired some dry clothes - using a downstairs guest bathroom to change - while soup was had among the Cuddly Nook guests and Misses Ridgeway. The rain lessened but did not go away. The lightning flashed more frequently. Tookis suggested that he and Avery leave but Avery took one look out the window and said, "Our house can wait. Let's wait it out here so we stay dry."

Misses Ridgeway said to them both, "I have a spare room upstairs for the two of you. And a room for Mister Abieris, and one for Pat. Which reminds me - " she slowly rose out of her seat. "I need to go upstairs and get some beds ready."

"Here, let me help you," Pat said, rising to her feet.

Blue also got up. "Hey Avery, can I chat with you for a second? In the kitchen." Relying on his cane a little more than usual - the storm outside made his bones ache - he and the small capuchin man retreated to the back of the house.

After a few minutes, Avery emerged but Blue did not. He cut through the dining room on the opposite side of the house to go upstairs. Roisin noticed this and thought it a little suspicious, but said nothing.

During dinner, the guests spoke among themselves, even as the storm quieted then swelled again. Once in a while, thunder would boom and make Tookis, the biggest among them, jump a little in his seat. His tail bristled each time. Roisin found it endearing, in a way, to see a big, tough guy afraid of storms.

Roisin would steal glances over at Fuloos. She would see him chatting, but as soon as the attention fell away from him, he would droop in his seat and let his eyes fall to the floor. It hurt to see him so, especially since she knew his home - his ancestral home - was being battered and beaten by the storm outside.

After a while, she got up and sat next to him. Neither said a word, but Fuloos noticed her, and he sat up straighter and looked at the others more. This was enough for her.

Then, Blue poked his head around the edge of the kitchen door. "Roisin," he asked, "could you come here for a second please?"

When she got to the kitchen, she saw Misses Ridgeway's silver tray with a fresh pot of tea, a small array of cups, and a sugar basin, all looking familiar to her.

"Are these..." she said. "Are these from Fuloos' house?"

Blue held up a finger to insist she stay quiet. "Can you carry this out for me please? It's too heavy for me to do one-handed."

And then Roisin's heart skipped a beat. For she realized the truth about Blue that had been staring her in the face the whole time. For it wasn't that Blue hated spending time with people - it just wasn't how he showed affection. He showed affection with gifts. She realized, too, that she didn't despise the gifts he gave. Just that the best ones for her were when he spent time with her. And here Blue stood in the kitchen, with a tea tray of Fuloos' things - a gift of normalcy after an evening of upheaval.

She gladly picked up the tray and carried it to the living room.

Upon seeing Fuloos' face, she smiled even brighter. The bird man carefully reached for a mug - a sea-green one. The same one he drank from when he gave comfort to Roisin yesterday. "Is..."

Blue stepped into the kitchen entryway, leaning on the doorframe instead of his cane. "I asked Avery to dig out some of your things so we could have some tea. He uh..." He reached to the island counter behind him and picked up an aging cookbook. "He mentioned that your mom and grandparents made tea, and they had a blend for the broken-hearted. I mixed it the best I could. I hope it turned out ok."

Fuloos didn't speak right away. He closed his eyes and took a deep breath in, his shoulders trembling in spite of himself.

Roisin sat next to him and held her arms around his shaking shoulders in a warm hug. For in her epiphany, she knew that touch meant so much to him.

And Misses Ridgeway - for her act of love - served the tea.

*

Fuloos lived in an apartment across the street from the Cuddly Nook, with two new roommates.

The day after the storm, he and a handful of others, including Blue and Roisin, took a look at the wreckage. The entire cave house had been flooded, furniture either destroyed or washed out completely, belongings left inside ruined with waterlog and dead fish. There had been no sign of Star during the trip.

Blue had unpacked his camera from his luggage and brought it with him, to photograph the aftermath. He had taken pictures the day before with the Cuddly Nook crew - the Nookies, Avery coined - to balance things out. Blue also took photos during the Storm Recovery fundraiser the Earth Church put together within the week. Ylas and Havith liked the photos and suggested Blue take them to the Coffee Haus, to see if Burt would hang them on the walls. Burt needed the art, the Earth Church wanted their work known, and Blue had been eager to get more photography work.

Roisin had canceled her return trip ticket, and hence commenced a series of events that cemented her place and Blue's among the residents of Seabank. They quit their city jobs, found an apartment across from the Cuddly Nook, and let the previous apartment lease expire. Roisin had insisted that this situation had been "temporary, until we're sure Fuloos will be ok."

Fuloos still kept writing and running his radio show. He had been scheduled to do an interview the day after the storm, but the segment turned into coverage of the storm's aftermath. That, in turn, caused an outpouring of support from sister cities like Treeta. The following months had been a flurry of activity, from beach clean-ups to house repairs for those folks who lived closer to the sea. This had included Gurthie, who had to delay her winter trip due to the damage to her home. Blue had insisted on co-hosting a photography show at the Coffee Haus, where sales of the art on the walls could benefit Gurthie and her recovery. The show had raised enough to cover repairs, at least.

Roisin had retired from modeling, and had taken up post as one of Ingrid's helpers at Jenny's during the day, then working in the Mayor's offices on the weekends, advocating for preserving old languages, including Faiji, the whistling language the community used. Fuloos, Avery, and Pat had taught her some phrases, and soon she had acquired enough skill to whistle basic announcements, warnings, and calls. She had started teaching some classes with Havith at the Earth Church, to teach younger people how to use the whistles.

Fuloos continued writing. He thought he had lost his book acquisitions for his biography of Chief Olohoolu - until Roisin came home one day, saying, "Ingrid kept asking when you were going to come back for these. So I just brought them for you." He gave her the biggest hug that day.

On this day, he had been jotting down his final thoughts for this book's epilogue when he heard the door open and shut.

He looked up from the kitchen table. "Hi, Blue," he said, smiling. "Good day?"

"VERY good day," said Blue, slipping the camera and its strap off from around his neck. "I think the Mayor's gonna' like these once they develop." He had just come back from the renaming ceremony for the town train station. The community had agreed to change the name once it had been discovered that it had been named for someone with Gold Talon sympathies. It had been renamed to Jufi Pass Train Station, after the Buteo Ja word for "friend."

Blue approached the table. "Did you finally finish the draft?"

"Almost. Just one more thought..." Fuloos picked up the pen and scribbled quickly.

As he did, Blue came over and gave him a scratch on the back - in just the right spot where he always itched after sitting so long. Fuloos closed his eyes in bliss. "Thank you. I needed that."

"Mmhmm." Blue stepped into the kitchen. He didn't have to go far - just a step or two. The apartment had been larger than the one Blue and Roisin had in Inlai, but not by much. At least they had an in-unit washer and dryer instead of a communal laundry situation, which Roisin absolutely loved. Blue and Fuloos heard the timer for the dryer go off in the back of the apartment.

Blue said, "I'm gonna' make some tea to celebrate the good day." He turned his feathered head around and asked, "Did Roisin say if she was staying late?"

"Not today. But I wouldn't be surprised if she did."

Blue nodded. They both knew Roisin loved working at Jenny's, even if it didn't pay very much. She had become the resident expert on Biographies and Local History. She had even read local authors outside of Fuloos's work.

About an hour into tea and catching up, Roisin came through the door. "Hey!"

"She's home!" Blue cheered, his crest feathers rising.

"We have tea," said Fuloos.

"Question - " said Roisin. "Will it pair well with..." she lifted a paper grocery bag in her hands. She always got paper bags so the children at the Earth Church had crafting materials she could donate. "Noodles?"

The crest feathers on both men's heads perked up. Blue had to ask, "Is it from Yili Yili?"

"Jeff yeah it's from Yili Yili!" Yili Yili was the noodle bar Havith's sister, Tethi, started with other Rabbithop youth. The place quickly became known for the best noodles and fry-bread in town.

The trio set up the take-out and their plates, and all three gathered around the table - a gift from Pat when they moved in - and caught up with each other over dinner.

Fuloos felt in that moment the reality of his life sink in. He had lost his ancestral house. He lost many things that had been left behind in that house. But he was alive. He still had some belongings - his mother's cookbook, his grandfather's mugs, one of the plates his grandmother had commissioned from her artist friend (the rest had broken in one of the trucks, but he kept the shards, as Roisin insisted she could make something new with them). The presence of those things helped the loss of the house hurt less.

Of course he still felt the grief. The grief of a lost house - a lost connection to a long-gone family, whom he still missed sometimes. And yet, he was home, here, with Blue and Roisin. The promise of making a new family with these two was a gift he could not ignore.

Roisin, who pulled him from the sea after he made his most foolish mistake, saved his life, and held his hand the whole evening. And Blue, who gave him a gift he never forgot - a sense of peace and home in the middle of a storm.

He would never forget the stories told to him from his ancestors. But he also looked forward to the stories he would make, with the people he loved most.

ACKNOWLEDGEMENTS

This book was a labor of love that I mostly did in secret. But there are some people who helped push this book to the edge to finally make it real.

First, thank you to C. Beranek and Kai Carter, my beta readers who gave valuable feedback when the story was still a work in progress.

Next, thank you to the Toledo Arts Commission for taking the chance with this book and giving the gift of an Accelerator Grant to get it to print. I hope that the community of Toledo loves this book as much as I loved writing it.

Thank you to the patrons on Ko-Fi and KickStarter for your support of this book. I know this is not like my usual projects. Thank you for trying something new with me.

And last, but never least - thank you to the best friends I could ask for: Alex Peterson, Chloe Rose, Lyn and "Sunshine" Cooley, Sean McGavin, and Ben Wright-Heuman.

Thank you, as well, to the community that's sprung up around me, including but not limited to: Gary, Brittany, Jeremy, Rainer, Angela, Alex W, the amazing folks of the Columbus Cartoon Coalition, including Sydney and JM, the folks at the Cartoonist Co-op and the Heatsink Comics Collective, and the Rossford Public Library and the Toledo Lucas County Public Library.

I also want to acknowledge the inspiration for many elements of this story. Shout-out to The Book Loft of Columbus, OH. You're the inspiration for Jenny's bookstore. Special thanks, as well, to the Navajo Nation and Hopi people for inspiring the indigenous people of Fwishi'shi. And a very special thank you to the peoples the world over who use and preserve the real whistled languages that inspired the one in this book.

Finally, thank you to my grandmothers, who were the inspiration for Misses Breanne Ridgeway. May you rest in peace. Also, yes, she is named after my cat, BreeBree, the real queen of the house.

www.ingramcontent.com/pod-product-compliance
Lightning Source LLC
Chambersburg PA
CBHW030539180626
46810CB00005B/1931